MISTRESS OF MELTHORPE

MISTRESS OF MELTHORPE

Alan Bloom

AIDAN ELLIS

First published in the United Kingdom by
Aidan Ellis Publishing, Cobb House, Nuffield,
Henley on Thames, Oxon RG9 5RT

First edition 1996

A CIP catalogue record for this book is available from the British Library

Typeset in Plantin by
The Midlands Book Typesetting Company,
Loughborough, Leics LE11 1HH
Printed in Britain by Biddles Ltd, Guildford, GU1 1DA

ISBN: 0 85628 272 3

Also by Alan Bloom:

The Farm in the Fen (1944)
The Fens
Hardy Perennials
Selected Garden Plants
Skaters of the Fens
Perennials for Trouble Free Gardening
Alpines for Trouble Free Gardening
Moisture Gardening
Hardy Plants of Distinction
Alpines of Distinction
Perennials in Island Beds
Faber Book of Traction Engines
The Bressingham Story
Prelude to Bressingham
Plantsman's Progress
Perennials for Your Garden
Alpines for Your Garden
Steam Engines at Bressingham
250 Years of Steam
A Plantsman's Perspective
Reeds in the Wind
The Story of Bressingham
Hardy Perennials (A Life with Plants)
Steam Alive
Garden Alpines
Come You Here, Boy! (1995)

Chapter One

'Berkeley will have to go,' Gerald said in a quieter than usual tone of voice, after several tense minutes as he tried to overtake a large high lorry on the all too narrow A11 south of Thetford. Anne had come to accept that such blunt statements of his intentions meant that he'd made up his mind already but was willing to hear her views and then give his reasoned arguments which left no room for change or compromise.

Until quite recently she would have concurred or demurred with what she considered intelligent remarks, still trusting to his superior judgment on other than purely domestic matters which he considered to be her domain. But Tom Berkeley was on a six month mutual trial as head gardener at Melthorpe Manor and Anne had only vague reasons for hoping he would stay on. With much less than half the trial period gone by, it startled her out of the dull mental lethargy which she felt every Tuesday morning as they returned for their three-day weekly residence in London. To leave Melthorpe on a bright May morning made what was becoming an irksome routine even more of a burden for her.

'Why?' she asked, choking back a sudden unexpected surge of emotion and deciding to let him explain without the deferential promptings she was expected to offer.

'Because I don't think he's our type of gardener – or maybe I should add, not right for our type of garden.' Gerald's voice regained the usual resonance which over the twenty-four years of their marriage had encouraged her to speak in soft, low tones.

'You're surely not dissatisfied with the pace he works at, are you? And from what I've noticed, he keeps Trevor and Michael on the job far more than Hicks managed to do.'

'You misunderstand me Anne,' Gerald explained, adopting a somewhat hurt tone as if she were trying to put him off balance. 'He works quite hard, as gardeners go these days, but you know perfectly well that tradition means a lot to me. Hicks was a good example of the old school, giving us masses of colour for spring, summer and autumn by seasonal bedding out. Except for the war years, Hicks has been upholding the Edwardian tradition I determined to restore when I bought the manor in 1945. It may not be the cheapest form of gardening, but for me it's far and away the best and as you know by now I'm willing to pay for what I believe in. And I still believe our lovely house, which is more your department, needs the kind of garden I've insisted on. And I don't think Berkeley has that kind of incentive to be a success here, in spite of what he told me at the interview.'

Gerald had been leaning forward over the Jaguar's steering wheel as he spoke, casting quick glances towards Anne. Now he leaned back settling his broad shoulders into the seat back as if waiting for her to accept his ruling. On his heavily jawed face was the kind of smile which Anne had only lately seen as smug. She guessed that he had more to say on the subject of Tom Berkeley if she said anything else in his favour.

'I suppose you'll let him stay the six months agreed on?'

'Of course! I'm not in the habit of going back on an agreement even if it's only verbal. I'll give him plenty of time to find another place — and besides I'll need time to find a replacement. I'll say nothing to him for another month or so, and that goes for you too, my dear.'

A silence fell as they passed over the chalky hill beyond Barton Mills. Once through the speed restrictions at Red Lodge, Gerald spoke again, reverting to his quieter tone. 'I noticed you and Berkeley were in what appeared a confidential discussion yesterday. I could see you through my study window when I happened to look up from the papers I was dealing with. What was it about darling?'

Ever since Gerald's first announcement Anne had suspected that this might crop up. She had taken her usual after-breakfast walk in the two acre garden hoping again Tom would be out of sight from the house when she came across him at work with or without his two young helpers. She had come to enjoy a brief chat with him. Awkward and halting though he often was in conversation, she felt a peculiar kind of sympathy for him knowing that he must be suffering from a sense of failure in life. He had applied for the job, he'd admitted, because after two years as a nurseryman on his own account he'd been obliged to go back to private service in order to make a living. His wife was a native of Melthorpe village and after twenty years absence was content to return now that their daughter had left home.

Anne had met Tom carefully hoeing amongst a bed of wallflowers and tulips within one of the encircling low-clipped box hedges, and during the next ten minutes he confessed that he had a problem and hoped she could help to solve it. She was aware that they could be seen from the house almost a hundred yards away, and was on edge as he said he needed a little plot till autumn in which to lay in some choice plants he had rescued from his nursery in Surrey. The tied cottage Gerald had offered him had a tiny garden and having filled all its available space needed more. His hope was that in return for a temporary plot in the large manor kitchen garden, he would willingly give some to make a border of perennials come autumn – whether or not he stayed on, as he hoped he would be asked to do.

A very reasonable request, Anne thought, but she had to explain that her husband would be the one to decide.

A wry smile had come over Tom's weathered features as he stood tall and spare-framed with one hand on the end of the now upright hoe shaft. 'Well, then, I'll have to ask him. Or would you?' he asked.

Anne had given a little laugh devoid of mirth. 'Give me a day or two,' she said feelingly. 'I'll think about it and hopefully come up with an answer when we come back from London on Friday. If it's any help meantime I can tell you I'm all in favour. This garden needs more variety and I could become quite interested in your special plants. But I doubt we'll convert the major.'

The title itself, as well as what it stood for, had become devalued for her over the years. Never more so than now as she struggled to hold down her feelings. She knew Gerald well enough to guess that his seemingly casual enquiry was motivated by suspicion in keeping with his dominance over her. Torn between making a rebellious outburst and the need for calm so as to meet Tom's request, the issue was settled by Gerald breaking in on her delay in answering.

'I'd like to know,' he said coldly, 'what that little tête-a-tête was about Anne. Can't you be open about it – if it was all above board?'

'It was,' she snapped, 'but I've had as much as I can take of your domineering. You've no right –.'

Gerald had suddenly jammed on the brake to avoid hitting the rear of a car which had cut in ahead. It put an end to what else was boiling up to say as she lurched forward. 'Bloody idiot!' Gerald muttered. 'But what you said was enough to make me lose concentration – if not control. What's got into you Anne? You've never spoken to me like that before, and I hope you never will again. I'll let it pass for now but maybe we'd best have a talk this evening and sort out what seems to be a problem you have. I can't bear to think of you being unhappy.'

With the shock of a near accident followed by Gerald subsiding into conciliatory tones and remarks, Anne's anger was replaced by realism. She could achieve nothing, neither freedom nor rights as a person, by open challenge, however much this might relieve her feelings. It had come almost in a flash of insight that far better results would come from using similar methods as Gerald, to be more of a schemer to gain her still hazy ideas of freedom and independence. She could begin by playing on the hurt tone in his voice.

'There's no need to be suspicious Gerald. Tom has a problem and was asking my advice on how best to approach you. I guess he's a wee bit afraid of you.' Anne gave a false laugh as if Tom's predicament was of no deep concern to her, adding that with all the garden space there was, Tom's request was a trivial matter, easily disposed of at no inconvenience.

Tensed as she was it came as a surprise when Gerald's left hand gave her knee a little pat. 'Feminine instinct,' he chuckled, 'wanting to help lame dogs over stiles without questioning motives and all that. Did you think to remind him, for example, that he shouldn't bank on being here much longer?'

'No, but he did say he hoped you would keep him on. But if not, he would leave some plants for a border and take the rest away. To me, it seemed a very fair offer. Don't you agree?'

'Hm!' Gerald snorted. 'I'd wager there's more to it than that which you, my dear, would never suspect. But you know me – it's in my nature to analyse and I'd say he's offering the thin edge of a wedge. If those plants mean so much to him, he's either holding on to them to start up on his own again, or maybe persuade me to let him use them to change the character of the garden. That's something I will not allow and that's the reason he'll have to go. After reading that press report last year, about it being a unique garden with a feast of colour, I'm all the more determined to keep to my own ideas. Raising over £2,000 for charity from six public openings shows it's appreciated. People can go to Blickling or Bressingham if they want to see a lot of herbaceous borders and such like.'

'So you'll turn down Berkeley's request?' Anne said quietly, reverting to the surname which Gerald invariably used for employees, despite the envy she suspected he felt of Tom's posh surname compared with his own plebien inheritance.

'You're jumping the gun again old dear. All I've said was to point out snags you may not have seen. By the time we come back at the weekend, I may well think up some safeguards and let him have an out of the way plot for his precious plants.'

'I hope so,' Anne added softly. 'I take your point, but I just feel rather sorry for him. Perhaps he's a born loser.' She wished she could have added, 'I've begun to feel I'm one myself', but was in no mood to meet the fresh challenge which such a remark would evoke. He would remind her, as he'd done so often before, that she was a vital part of his existence as his wife and the mistress of Melthorpe – apart from bearing him a son and daughter. The fact was that no matter how she'd chided herself for not having a strong maternal instinct, it made no difference except to leave her with a certain sense of guilt. Her inclinations as well as her beliefs were centred more on duty.

She had loved her children, Julian and Susan, and still did, but not in a possessive way. Nor did she lavish outward affection on them. Her protectiveness and care for them had, along with her nurturing influence, diminished as they grew up. They should be encouraged, she believed, to become persons in their own right and this attitude had fitted in with Gerald's own ideas and his business commitments.

Gerald Potts was one of several partners in the London based firm of estate agents, Wroxley, Ross and Partners, specialists in upper crust London and Provincial residential properties. Their advertisements regularly occupied four pages of 'Country Life'. His father had also been in the firm as a solicitor in charge of Searches and Conveyancing and Gerald was given a good start on leaving Westminster School in 1934 at the age of eighteen. His wartime experiences in requisitioning property for military purposes with rapid promotion gave added proof of his shrewdness and rectitude. And on being accepted into the partnership he proudly stood up for conservatism in the British way of life, with moral values its bulwark.

Having bought Melthorpe Manor with its 370 acres, he set about restoring the handsome Queen Anne period house with loving care, moving in with his widowed mother with still more work to be done. But by 1953 he was ready to find a suitable wife, his mother promising to make way for her with no hard feelings. By then he was well into his thirties and as a respected, not unhandsome specimen of real manhood, his roving eye had widespread scope.

Gerald's choice fell on Anne Webley, only daughter of a progressive farmer living three miles from Melthorpe. James Webley was widely known as a campaigner for rural welfare with both the Farmers Union and Norfolk County Council as his platform. Some of his friends marvelled at his indefatigable energy and how he managed to have such a model farm whilst spending so much time and thought outside its boundary. It was, however, not a large farm and it had been James's deliberate choice to make the most of its 150 acres rather than expand as so many had when land was cheap to buy or rent. His one son, Brian, was somewhat reluctantly trained to eventually take over and Anne helped with records and bookkeeping whilst fully active with the local Young Farmers Club, until one day Major Gerald Potts called to ask her father's advice on matters concerning his own farm. That day was not long after Anne's eighteenth birthday and eighteen months later she was mistress of Melthorpe Manor.

Anne believed herself at the time to be a very fortunate young lady. Both her parents had said so, whilst stressing her need to defer to Gerald in view of both his social position and of his being fifteen years her senior. She had in fact been nurtured, especially by her mother, to look up to men as the superior sex, and she had done so to bring a close relationship with her father. 'It's the sure recipe for a happy marriage and the way to wifely fulfilment, with children the natural outcome as a seal and a blessing,' her mother assured her again on the morning of her wedding.

People remarked as the happy couple posed for the cameras beside Melthorpe church porch, on what a fine looking couple they were. Gerald, though heavily built, was only a shade taller than Anne. Her contrasting slimness was just right. His face was oval in shape with brown eyes under thick brows and receding black hair, whereas Anne's rounded, wide-jawed features were in contrast with her low forehead topped by somewhat curly honey-coloured hair. The contrast in their experience of life, however, was a matter for Gerald to rectify.

And Anne was willing enough to come under his tutelage, to learn more about the social graces and to play her full part in living up to what Gerald expected of her as his wife. His way with her was one of gentle, respectful insistence, whether for a social occasion and how the household should run, or how she dressed. And the fears she had of his being over-demanding in his nuptial rights in bed were dispelled when the time came. Sex, he explained weightily, was an appetite, and like any other should not be debased by excessive indulgence.

It was at weekends that such intimacies mostly occurred. Gerald usually went to London twice a week by train, but was often off early in the morning by car to inspect a property in East Anglia or the adjoining shires. During the first year of their marriage, Anne sometimes went with him on these inspections and they occasionally stayed overnight at an hotel. But as she discovered that he preferred not to talk about his business concerns, she found it increasingly difficult to find a reliable basis for companionship as he steered the conversation on to topics of interest to himself – politics, economics, workpeople's attitudes, the state of the nation and the dismemberment of the British Empire, and cricket.

When Anne first knew she was pregnant, ambivalent thoughts assailed her. It would be some relief to keep her home-bound, but she feared the responsibility of nurturing Gerald's child and in failing to experience any great thrill of anticipation of being a mother. Feelings of guilt which this evoked were sharpened by Gerald's hope for a son, and the money he lavished on her as the bearer of his heir. From the very first he had been generous in what he gave her for personal and household use, but now she was pregnant nothing was too good for her and no expense was to be spared. Julian arrived, after a long and difficult labour, but Gerald was a very proud father indeed. So much so that before Julian began to crawl Anne was pregnant again.

Anne dare not tell Gerald the real reason why she preferred not to have a nanny until the babies were older. She could easily manage, she said, with Mrs Wells as cook/housekeeper and a daily from the village. But when Susan was four, Gerald insisted Julian and she must go to the nearest kindergarten school at Attleborough since it was time Anne resumed her interrupted social life with him. He announced that he had bought a first floor flat in Chelsea and there they would stay for two or three days most weeks of the year.

Torn both ways as she was, Anne found she had no course open than to concur. She was becoming unsure of herself, who she really was, and which of the roles she was expected to play to lead to a better prospect of fulfilment. Children were not surely the be-all for her existence, nor was her place as Gerald's consort with its superficialities. She was a dyed-in-the-wool country woman and yet not even the attractions of Melthorpe Manor, house, garden, farm and woods meant very much to her. It was all so much Gerald's domain and for all her knowledge of farming he seldom discussed such matters with her, leaving management almost entirely to his two foremen in charge of livestock and cultivations. So it was that Anne fell in with Gerald's new plan without saying she would have preferred to stay behind at Melthorpe. She was his wife and it was her duty to follow his lead. It was up to her to make the best of life as she found it and not kick against the pricks – as her parents had often reminded her when she felt frustrated. She had proved her ability as a hostess and housekeeper and Gerald never failed to commend her for it after some party was over and guests had departed. Quite often, however, his praise was not unqualified. When it ended with some remark on an apparently trivial fault or shortcoming on her part, it left her with the feeling that her efforts still fell below the high standards he expected. Now she'd got to do much more entertaining, she supposed, with London cocktail parties and theatre, which Gerald mentioned on noting her lack of enthusiasm when announcing the new departure from the Melthorpe routine.

Anne's initial misgivings on having to leave the children whilst she and Gerald were away in London were offset by his mother's readiness to stand in. She had moved out when Anne came to the manor and now lived with a widowed sister at Attleborough only five miles away. Gerald was so expert at fixing things that Anne had no valid complaint against his ordered way of life and this reinforced her resolve to fit in to the best of her ability. She disliked cocktail parties and the buzz of superficial, forced conversation, but enjoyed the theatre and Festival Hall concerts. She made a few desultory new friendships amongst the wives of Gerald's many business acquaintances. Some of these came to Melthorpe during the autumn and winter shooting season and it was very noticeable how, as a host and crack shot with a 12-bore gun, Gerald excelled in geniality and stability.

'That was most enjoyable,' he was wont to say when a party ended.

'Not least because you backed me up magnificently.' But very occasionally he would drop a gentle hint about her personal appearance. He was all in favour of her dressing smartly, to be seen and judged by other women as well as their men folk as tastefully elegant, with no superfluous finery except for his gifts of jewellery. At heart she preferred simplicity in what she wore, but she could not hurt him by saying so. On this score she worried about her figure and a tendency to put on weight. At thirty-five she was a stone heavier than when she married, and neither horse riding, exercising, massage or corsetry made much difference, partly because her weakness for eating titbits between meals was too hard to control.

Gerald's hints and innuendoes about her weight came with what she took as a tolerant smile. He too had put on several pounds over the years and he never went beyond saying 'so long as you never let yourself go fat and sloppy, and maybe we will both have to take ourselves in hand. We must keep up to scratch in our position, mustn't we?'

In due course both children went to first-class boarding schools and this made possible the cruise ship holidays which Gerald prescribed. His position in the firm was strong enough to afford the luxury of a holiday each summer seeing far-off places in style and comfort. Later on, when Julian and Susan were at Brazenose and Newnham respectively they took flights to Bermuda, Kenya or Kashmir, but Gerald always saw to it that they were back at Melthorpe when the garden was open to the public for charity. Although on these occasions, well advertised in the press, Anne preferred to serve teas or on the produce stall, whilst Gerald loved to mix with the visitors. He always carried a long, stout stick of polished holly wood, with a metal tip with which to prise out a weed here and there as he conducted chosen visitors round the garden. Visitors, however, were not to know that this exercise was the nearest he ever came to doing any manual work in the garden. More often than not his long stick was no more than an insignia, because old Hicks and his helpers were enjoined to keep the garden free of weeds for each of the weekends the visitors were allowed to see the feast of flowers and colour excelling, Gerald believed, any other garden in Norfolk.

Anne saw such examples of her husband's egoism, as harmless. Nor did she ever question the source of his wealth. She knew some of it came from playing the stocks and shares market, because the

Financial Times was so important to him before, during and after breakfast. Being so free as she was of any worry where money was concerned, it did sometimes occur to her as a snare which her secret donations to famine relief and the like eased her guilty feelings only a little. Most of these feelings however arose because life for all its pleasure and day to day concerns seemed at times rather empty and futile. She believed in the Christian ethics but some of the truths lying behind the parables of Jesus, such as that of the Talents, the Sower and the Rich Man left her uneasy. She herself had done so little towards either self-denial or self-development leading to the abundance of life which Jesus proclaimed. The pattern of her life, she decided on reaching forty, had been woven by Gerald. There was no positive, or possible way in which she could change it. In their early days together she had made suggestions about minor improvements to the house and other matters in which she felt she should be concerned. But always there came the indulgent but superior smile – even before she'd completed her piece, which with experience told her he was not even listening to what she had to say. And if he was never ill-tempered or angry with her, it was, she came to reflect rather ruefully, that she had never given him cause or provocation.

It was soon after Anne's fortieth birthday that her brother Brian was killed in a car crash. No one who knew the way he drove his Capri was surprised, but everyone's sympathy went out to his father whose secret fears had become a reality. It was so unfair. Anne and Brian had been quite good friends, but she grieved intensely that such a kindly, industrious man should have a son who was so lacking in responsibility. Brian had never married and settled down and much preferred to be foot loose and fancy free. And although Anne now realised she might well, in due course, be the owner of Dunsford Farm as the only surviving child, the prospect was inconsequential at the time. James Webley sought solace in driving himself harder than ever with a seemingly stoic determination to transcend his tragic loss, as if he believed it was for the best, an act of Providence, and kept up the pace of work and service for three more years before suffering a heart attack which ended his life within three weeks. When his will was revealed Anne was left the farm with provision for her mother. It would be Anne's responsibility to provide her with other acceptable accommodation if she so desired. Provision had also been made for enough income for the remainder of her life and this left Anne nothing but the bare freehold of the 150 acre farm, the house and two cottages.

'With land prices still rising,' Gerald said as the expert, 'it's worth well over a hundred thousand. And my advice is to sell it while the going's good. Why not let me handle it for you and re-invest the money? I could get you more for it than anyone – and an income way above what you'd get in rent if you let it. Come to that, we could easily work such an acreage, only three miles away, in with my own farm and that might be your best bet. If your mother wants a smaller house for herself I could fix that for her, and the farmhouse could be sold off separately at a very good price. Think about it, my dear, but don't mention my suggestions to anyone else. You know you can trust me to do the best for you, don't you? So what's your first reactions to what I've said?'

'Oh, I don't really know,' Anne replied, squirming inside as she hesitated. 'I'm still a bit dazed. I've not become fully aware that Dad's gone and it's early days to talk about what to do with the farm. Mother's future has to come first and she can't be expected to make up her mind yet.'

Gerald's approach took place only a week after the cremation and it struck Anne as being premature to say the least. Perhaps what she'd said had made him realise that he had been somewhat imprudent or insensitive in making such suggestions during the worst period of her grief. But he would not know the effect that had on her, except that her silence on the subject during the weeks that followed was enough to put him off mentioning it again. Her father had died early in April, only a fortnight after Tom Berkeley had come to work in the garden. Gerald's attitude on that score had added to the hurt he had caused her over the future of Dunsford Farm and now both matters were rankling as one, to which other facets of her situation and Gerald's domination were stirring and bubbling up in her mind. She had, in fact, become increasingly intrigued with the notion of taking on the farm herself with the help of the foreman Ted Fletcher, who lived in one of the two cottages. The thought offered a gleam of hope that by so doing and braving Gerald's almost inevitable opposition, she could assert her own independence to become a person in her own right and not just a support for Gerald's own image of himself.

Chapter Two

Tom Berkeley had, they said, no proper ambition. Both his brothers and his father upbraided him for wanting to be just a gardener and that was no job for anyone wishing to get on in the world. Geoff and Harold were mechanically minded and went into the Dennis works at Guildford where their father was a foreman. But when Tom left school in 1945 at sixteen he was quite content to work at Jackmans nursery near Woking for thirty shillings a week. As a beginner he was given such menial jobs as weeding, mixing potting soil and scrubbing clay pots. In season he helped to dig up shrubs and plants for orders and when one day Roland Jackman spoke to him about his work and his future, Tom was thrilled and worked harder than ever. Roland Jackman was a kindly man and, having explained how the recent war had affected nursery stocks, he had asked Tom if he would like to help with propagating perennials and alpines which had become so scarce through wartime stringencies.

Taking cuttings, making divisions and transplanting seedlings was for Tom fascinating work, and on winter evenings he studied any catalogues and books he could lay his hands on. The Latin names of plants became less and less of an obstacle to him and it intrigued him to discover little by little how immense was the range of plants, even just the hardy ones which appealed most to him. At home his devotion was rather a joke. Only his mother stood up for him when brothers and father made fun of him for being rather a sissy compared with their own attitude to work and spending the good money they earned. Like their father, Geoff and Harold were brawny, one taking up boxing and the other rugger as recreations. But Tom had no need, he said, for such recreations and though tall and thin was more disposed to let off energy with a spade or hoe in the home garden.

The dreaded call-up for National Service came and there was no exemption for Tom as there had been for Geoff and Harold. He hated the life in uniform with its waste of time and effort. But as his maternal grandfather had advised – he had survived the horrors of the trenches in the 1914 war – 'What can't be cured must be endured'.

To a large extent it was sound sense, Tom discovered, and apart from becoming physically tough and mentally grim under overbearing authority, he found some solace in caring for what went as gardens around the Officers Mess, both at Colchester and in Germany. When his two years ended he went back to Jackmans, longing to become again immersed in plants. But Roland Jackman advised him against it. There was, he explained, no vacancy at the level of skill Tom would have reached but for National Service. Rather than begin again lower down, it would be far better to go in for a Diploma Course at Wisley Gardens, to become thereby more of an all-rounder. Roland smoothed the way for Tom and, although he learned a lot about some aspects of horticulture he had no wish to pursue, Wisley gave him ample opportunity to study the realm of decorative hardy plants under Ken Aslet and the rather formidable Mr Hammer. Even if only weeding the Rock Garden and staking and furbishing the long herbaceous borders, every kind of plant became to Tom a living subject with almost personal characteristics.

At twenty-two, with an RHS Diploma, Tom was in two minds about his future. He was offered a propagator's job at Jackmans, but their range of perennials and alpines had become more limited. Demand, Roland Jackman explained, had veered more towards shrubs as being less troublesome for garden owners now that labour saving was such a big consideration. Other alternatives were to go to a specialist hardy plant nursery – of which there were now fewer than before the war – or to a Botanic Garden such as Kew, there to become more of a specialist himself, which might lead to an assistant curatorship. He went for an interview at Kew and there he met Shirley. Tom had avoided girls except when with others in army uniform. There was a vivacity about Shirley that appealed to him. That appeal grew to such an extent that when he became one of the second grade staff a fortnight later, he felt she was the only person he knew there that really mattered to him. Her lodgings were not far from his own, and whereas he had reckoned on spending most of his evenings studying, there was now every incentive not to do so when hers were free.

Shirley, a brown-eyed slim-figured blonde, told him that she'd come to the big city when she was seventeen to get away from village life in Norfolk. Now, five years later with half a dozen different waitressing and hotel jobs behind her, she was glad to be at least on the edge of the country rather than in London itself. She liked meeting people and that was why she preferred her kind of job to one in a shop or office. But she'd never met anyone like Tom before, a sentiment which he could endorse for himself, and having savoured the physical side of their mutual attraction to each other, Tom's ambitions took on a new and exciting prospect. They were so obviously made for each other and Shirley needed no persuasion to marry him.

For several months they shared a bed-sitter. Shirley found a day time job in a nearby hotel whilst Tom continued working in Kew Gardens. But after a year, when Shirley was sure she was pregnant, they decided they needed a house and she persuaded him to apply for a gardener's job where one was provided. With his Diploma and a reference from Jackmans and the Curator of Kew Gardens, the first advertisement he responded to led to an engagement. It was at nearby Cobham, and the gardener's cottage in the three acres of woods and garden was well nigh idyllic. To be a private gardener had never been one of Tom's limited ambitions, but with an elderly part-timer to help he felt sure he would find no lack of satisfaction in caring for his stockbroker employer's garden, which had been first designed by no less a notable than Gertrude Jekyll.

They chose Sandra for their baby's name. Tom adored her and even persuaded Shirley to let him bath her and change her nappies. Life took on a new dimension, but if it gave him a twinge of regret to hear Shirley say she wanted no more babies and was keen to go out to work again, he conceded that this was her right.

'We could do with the extra money, couldn't we?' Shirley was inclined to argue as if, after all, she was not quite satisfied with her lot. Evidence of this came when Sandra showed she had a will of her own from a very early age, and when the first slaps came from Shirley they hurt Tom as well. 'I'm not going to let her rule our lives,' Shirley protested. 'And she's got to learn when I say no I mean it. You'd spoil her if you had your way Tom, and I can't have that either now or when the time comes for me to go out to work again. Your wages won't pay for the fridge and washing machine I need, will they?'

'They pay for your cigarettes,' Tom defended mildly, 'and a few other things I didn't think we really needed for the home.' He hated strife and harsh words, but could not let her jibe pass without protest.

Although occasional tiffs and misunderstandings became more frequent and Sandra became more self-willed, Tom's ultimate attitude was to appease Shirley. He still loved her and, judging by her need of him in bed, she still loved him. One biblical saying had stuck in his memory from Sunday School days – 'Never let the sun go down on thy wrath'. It was a maxim well worth the effort it took to put into practice, especially with Shirley who was inclined to sulk if thwarted, leaving him with no alternative but to appease for the sake of the peace and goodwill which meant so much to him. There were times when he felt a kind of need to go to church again like he sometimes did before he left home for National Service. But he never did. Shirley not only enlisted his help with Sandra on a Sunday, and for other chores she found irksome, but scoffed at what she termed 'religious twaddle'.

Shirley's return to hotel work when Sandra was old enough for play school brought misgivings to Tom. He had been reared by parents who believed in family unity and integrity. His parents also believed that boys should be boys and girls truly feminine. But they had often made a joke about boys as snails and puppy dogs tails as their make-up and girls being spice and all things nice. His two sisters had been proud of Geoff and Harold because they were so masculine and manly, but were not allowed to tease Tom because of his shortcomings.

Tom had done his best and, although he knew he fell short of the family ideal of how the two sexes should be in contrast as opposites, they all showed an amused tolerance of his discrepancies. This, to a large extent, was offset by his physical strength and endurance which his lack of male aggressiveness did not match. The experience of having Shirley as wife and wilful Sandra as daughter brought him a sensitivity he had never been able to express before. He had sensed that his mother did not approve of his choice of a wife, and this made visits back home become rare occasions. He missed the hearty family atmosphere which he knew was based there, although all his siblings had now married and left home. And as time went on he came to realise more and more that he and Shirley were not after all made for each other.

It came as a shock to be told bluntly by Shirley that it was time he stopped giving Sandra the cuddles they both enjoyed. Sandra was then nine and still made a bee-line for him when he came in from work to flop on to his lap and relax as he stroked her blonde hair, or her bare arms. He had never seen this as harmful in the least, but as a perfectly natural thing, and means of showing mutual love and affection. But Shirley said she had hoped he would have the sense to realise that it was like playing with fire to fondle a child of Sandra's temperament. She herself had desisted because she'd found that petting from her and hugging from Sandra was so often a prelude to wheedling for some favour to be extracted by such means. But for a father to keep up what was all right in babyhood until a girl was as old and forward as Sandra, it could rouse sexiness in them both. 'It's the beginnings of incest can't you see that? And it doesn't go down at all well with me when you turn your back on me in bed, saying you're dog tired.'

He saw no alternative to putting a rather abrupt end to his closeness to Sandra. The expression in her eyes as he fumbled for excuses was hard to bear. But he was in no position to dispute with Shirley. Even if at heart he could see no harm in that means of showing affection for his only child, he could not ignore, much less defy Shirley. Automatically it generated a nagging resentment towards her, and her reference to his neglecting her in bed had the opposite effect on him. That same night, loaded as he was with an additional sense of guilt, he failed to get an erection when with a show of renewed affection towards him as if she had been too blunt, she fondled his privates but without result. 'Don't let it worry you,' she said softly. 'It'll come back, and I know what I said about you and Sandra must have come hard for you. I should have dropped the hint before, maybe.'

It took Tom hours of nagging worry before sleep came that night and for days it was uppermost in his mind, as a two pronged thrust into the deepest recesses of his mind. He saw himself as guilty on two more counts, adding to the lack of success in either his professional or his private life. At thirty-three he should have been at his prime in every respect, but instead he was shackled by his own shortcomings and with a wife who, he was slowly coming to realise, was inherently self-centred and insensitive. The 'what can't be cured must be endured' attitude to life returned with greater compulsion than ever.

For the next few years sex became a hit and miss affair and Sandra became more distant and more assertive of herself. And at fourteen she was using eye-shadow and the like at weekends. By this time Shirley's attitude towards her had become ambivalent. Sometimes she would talk to her as an equal woman of the world, offering advice on dress and giving her money to spend on herself. At other times her way would be nonchalant or dismissive as if to say it was up to her to choose her own way of life and that the sooner she was able to leave school and get a job, the better.

At the time, Shirley had a regular job at a country club type of hotel with its own golf course. After a year or two of travelling the five miles daily in the second-hand car which Tom had bought, she had money enough to buy her own. To some extent it was a relief to Tom for her to be away from home from midday to close on midnight. And although he did all he could to regain Sandra's confidence and show his affection for her in other than physical contact, she kept her distance and was seldom confiding. Nor was she any different, he noticed, towards her mother and seemed quite unconcerned that as a family they were far from united. Tom had ached inside at his isolation. It was bad enough while Sandra was still at school, but he dreaded the time when she would leave and make her own way in life. It was before she left school that she became friendly with a boy who owned a motorcycle.

One of the highlights in Tom's life as a gardener was to spend a whole day at Chelsea Show each year. Both this indulgence and his holidays alone visiting gardens once he owned a car became a vital outlet for his interest in the world of plants. It was also mental recreation after weeks of confinement within the boundary of his employer's garden. When he was away Shirley stayed at home with Sandra – if she was not also away on an organised school holiday. On the last of the latter just before her school life ended, Tom took off to visit some north country gardens, and although he had given up the habit of telephoning home, he did so on his first night away to ask Shirley to remedy an omission with orders he had left with his assistants. When he made his call late that evening to be sure of Shirley being at home, it was a man's voice who answered at ten p.m. before Shirley quickly took over.

Tom was so taken aback that he did no more than give her his message and hung up, as if he couldn't believe what he'd heard. Yet as the import sank in, he felt neither anger nor distress. Instead came a jumbled set of reactions. One of them was a kind of relief that in all probability some other man had taken his place, for he had himself become virtually impotent. That she had accepted the fact had not lessened his sense of failure and guilt, but now the guilt at least had suddenly become much less of a burden. That Shirley had been unfaithful did not upset him at all. It was nothing he could blame her for because he had long since wished he could have given up trying to satisfy her – and it wasn't after all entirely his fault. These thoughts made him feel strangely free at heart and having visited a small specialist nursery in Yorkshire, his old ambition of having one of his own came back with a rush.

With this uppermost in his mind he made no reference to the strange male voice over the telephone. Nor did Shirley, and to his surprise he found her quite solicitous as to how his holiday had gone. This prompted him to tell her about his thoughts, which brought another surprise. 'I'm all in favour,' she said blandly. 'You've been stuck in this job for long enough. A move might be good for Sandra too, but we mustn't be surprised if she gets a job where she can keep contact with her motorbike friends. She's got beyond our control now, more's the pity.'

It seemed as if Tom's luck had turned, for he found a little nursery for sale about as far south of Shirley's hotel as they were situated to the north. It was barely an acre in extent and the owner wished to retire from growing bedding plants and salads and a few indoor plants for local trade. The old man was willing to let half the £8,000 remain as mortgage, which left Tom, with Shirley's help, only two hundred to borrow from the bank, leaving also a few hundreds to buy in a nucleus of the kind of hardy plants in which he was so keen to specialise. Meantime, until these were built up into saleable quantities, he could carry on but gradually phase out the market garden crops.

Once moved and settled in, Tom worked as never before. His sense of purpose and joy at being his own boss offset his nagging personal anxieties. He knew, and Shirley guessed he knew, that she had another man – perhaps more than one, in her life. Sandra, as expected, obtained a job away from home in a supermarket at Esher where her friends lived, but made occasional visits of short duration saying all was going well for her.

At the end of the first year Tom displayed a notice to say that he had hardy plants for sale as an additional attraction to customers. But the few who came to see them took up precious time in having to be told what they were and why they cost so much more than the usual bedding plants. Salesmanship, Tom found, was not a gift that came easily to him, and it went against the grain when sometimes a customer took half an hour to select a pound's worth of plants. And it began to worry him that in cutting back on what the previous owner had grown and sold, the kinds of plants he himself preferred to grow were much less profitable. Money was becoming tight.

Two years after Tom began on his own, the previous owner died and his executors called for the mortgage to be repaid. Having studied his accounts, the bank decided to have nothing to do with it, especially as the overdraft they had allowed him had been only marginally reduced. All his hopes, so long deferred, began to deflate. He told himself and Shirley that if only he could have carried on for another year or so, all would have been well. There would have been enough stock and variety to catalogue and put up exhibits at flower shows as a means of obtaining orders. And then just as the balance of events began to weigh down against his being able to stage a recovery, Shirley announced that she was in deep trouble.

Tom did not probe her for details. It was shock enough, adding so much to his own depression, that she had been given instant dismissal. He knew it must be serious, especially when she said she'd trusted someone who badly let her down. Feeling too sorry for himself to feel genuine sorrow for her, he asked if she had any money left of her own.

'Not a cent,' she sighed tearfully. 'He took all mine as well.'

'I see,' hissed Tom, scarcely opening his lips. 'And I suppose you know I'm broke. I see no way out but to go back into private service well away from this area. But what about you? Can you get another job – I mean haven't you got some other contacts round here?'

'I don't want to stay round here either Tom.'

It was then he felt a twinge of sympathy for her. She was so deflated and although the prospect of having to share life with her again was not one he wished to foster, his renewed sense of failure brought back enough of his old sense of guilt to catch a glimpse of where his duty lay. After all, marriage was for better or worse. . .

Having put the nursery in the hands of a local estate agent he collected from the newsagents his Gardeners Weekly in which job vacancies were advertised. Shirley had stayed indoors and was tidying the house.

'I'll do some weeding or something if it'll help you,' she said calmly.

Tom made no comment except to say that his first priority now was to see what jobs were on offer. Five minutes later he called to her. 'Melthorpe – isn't that where you used to live?'

'Yes – why?'

'Because a Major Potts of Melthorpe Manor in Norfolk is advertising for a head gardener, with cottage available.'

Chapter Three

Within minutes of telling Shirley of the job vacancy at Melthorpe Manor, Tom realised that he'd fallen into a trap of his own making. Had he guessed what her reaction would be, he would have said nothing about it and responded to one of the other advertisements in the hope that from now on they would go their separate ways. There was nothing to hold them together and her predicament after all was not his responsibility morally or otherwise. She stood as good a chance of getting another job on her own as he did. But now she was bending over his shoulder to read the advertisement for herself.

'You will apply for it, won't you?' she said, giving him a friendly pat on the sleeve. 'There's nothing I'd like better than to be back home again. I've had enough of it down here and that's the truth. My Mum and Dad will be as pleased as Punch. I think we should stick together – turn over a new leaf, like.'

'There's a lot to consider,' Tom told her guardedly.

'I know, but the New Year has just begun and we've both got to get away from here, so let's keep together, shall we? I'm willing if you are, Tom.'

There was a ring of sincerity in her voice which he could not ignore. He knew that any job with a house provided would offer a refuge for a nucleus stock of the plants in which he had invested almost all of his savings. He would also be less likely to obtain a head gardener's job with a house and garden if he had no wife. Shirley, as if guessing his thoughts, said she'd do whatever she could to help him.

'And you could take some of your special plants and keep them in the cottage garden, couldn't you? The ad. doesn't say anything about wife doing part time housework, so that would leave me free to help you more, and I could look round for a job when we get settled. Do write straight away. Now you've sold your car you can have mine if they want you for an interview. I've heard Major Potts is well britched and not a bad chap to work for.'

Tom was well aware of being pushed, but saw no grounds for resistance. There was, so far as he could see, no other way to go, and two weeks later, against a bitter north east wind, he was on the A11 to Norfolk. The major left Tom in no doubt as to the kind of garden he was expected to maintain, as they walked round its many box-hedged paths and through the large kitchen garden, the lean-to vinery and the conservatory. He met Anne Potts only over tea and biscuits before setting off back to Surrey as darkness fell. But if there was little or no scope for the more varied range of plants with formality of Melthorpe, the major had at least told him he was free to bring a selection to fill, if need be, the garden of the cottage which he and Shirley would occupy.

'Six months trial,' the major insisted, 'and if there's mutual agreement to continue after that, I'd be happy to step up your wages. All right? Start in mid-March, by which time the house will be vacant.'

Tom felt he had little choice, but it rankled a bit that there had to be six month trial period when the major had said that his CV had been quite satisfactory, with his one post in private service lasting fifteen years.

The setting had appealed to Tom. Despite the day being cold and sunless, and the countryside rather flat, it was well wooded and the manor was sheltered with mature trees and wind breaks of holly and yew. The kitchen garden was walled on three sides with a red brick backing for the vinery and espalier fruits. There was direct access to the larger decorative garden on one side of the house, whilst on the other there were entrances to the lane which led to the village centre with its flint towered church.

The formal garden would demand much hedge clipping and there were many gravel paths to be kept tidy. It was in fact laid out geometrically, with circular, rectangular and diamond shaped beds edged with box, with a lavender hedged path across the large half-moon shaped lawn in front of the house. This led to a round area as a centrepiece with a sundial and rose pergola as cover to half hide an alcove with rustic seats.

Tom saw no alternative other than to fall in with Shirley's own way out. And even if he could not trust her new friendliness towards him, he could not muster what it would take to say so. To make the best of a bad job would be to follow her lead, to accept her at face value, but to retain his independence by avoiding intimacy with her.

On returning from his interview with Major Potts with the news that he'd got the job on a six month trial basis, Shirley was delighted. She dismissed his own misgivings about it not being his choice of a garden with all its formality.

'You'll be able to persuade him to change his ideas, I'm quite sure. You must take some of your special plants and when they flower in the cottage garden show him and I'll bet he'll want to buy some off you. And that'll be another feather in your cap – after you've shown him what a good gardener you are, he'll beg you to stay on beyond the six months. You'll see! And, just in case it's worrying you, I'll be content to be just your housekeeper. I mean, it's all right by me if you still want us to have separate bedrooms. We can still be good friends, can't we?'

It was as much in Tom's nature to believe what was spoken to him with apparent sincerity, as to choose words carefully in saying what he meant to convey. Shirley's remarks sunk in leaving more of an impression that she had undergone a change of heart since she lost her job at the hotel. It had become a habit to be reserved and to keep inner thoughts to himself, and perhaps he could face the future with less foreboding and allow room for hope.

'Okay then,' he conceded, 'and we should be at Melthorpe in eight weeks' time. If we can't find a buyer for this place by then we'll have to leave it to the agents. But I'll make sure there's nothing left behind I'll need to take, and I'll have to flog what plants I can't take to some nursery or garden centre. We'll need the money.'

There was a neglected stock of wooden trays left by the previous owner. These Tom mended and lined with paper as he systematically dug about ten each of the two hundred or so different kinds of plants he had acquired. Leaving some soil attached to the roots, he packed them upright in the trays, labelling each kind. Astilbes, cimicifugas, phlox and hostas were quite bulky and heavy and needed only a covering of peat to retain life till April if need be. Anemones, primulas, iris and the like were less heavy, and kinds grown in plastic pots needed more space but less protection. Every day while the weather remained good more trays were filled, often with Shirley's help, and when a frosty spell came late in February, there was some satisfaction for Tom in knowing the task was completed. A Woking dealer in nursery stock paid him two hundred pounds in cash for what had to be left behind – enough to pay for the lorry to move those going to Melthorpe.

March came with no firm offers for the property and this became Tom's greatest worry. Acting on Shirley's advice, the asking price was reduced and within a week a contract was signed at four hundred less than he'd paid for it. But as Shirley tartly pointed out, it wasn't really a loss because there was no stock in trade like there had been when he bought it.

With somewhat forced enthusiasm once the sale was agreed the move began. With their furniture in a van, the plants on a lorry, they headed the little convoy north, just in time for the major's deadline date.

Shirley's excitement was offset by Tom's despondent mood which she failed to dispel, and he couldn't tell her the reason for it. They had been asked to stay with her parents until the furniture was installed in their new home and Tom had found no valid excuse for refusing, on the grounds that he had no wish to share a bed with Shirley. She had made no mention of this, which left him with the certainty that her parents would expect them to do so. And because over the past weeks she had maintained her friendly helpful attitude, he could not muster what it would take to remind her of her willingness to accept his celibacy. During recent weeks he had an inkling that she hoped he would relent, but had shown no resentment as they went separately to their bedrooms. But now the trap he feared was about to close on him again, bringing the thought that it might all be a ploy on her part.

They were made very welcome by her parents and after a hearty supper, as the mantelpiece clock chimed ten, Shirley's father, a retired cowman, stood up to wind it. 'Ten o'clock's bedtime,' he said. 'I still get up at harpas six and you'll have a full day tomorrow, both of you.'

'And there's a hot water bottle in the bed,' his wife added with a broad smile as she too stood up.

An hour later, any hope that he would still be impotent with Shirley had vanished. She had chatted disarmingly as if to lull him to sleep after a tiring day, and then began to inch herself closer to him till he could feel her breasts touching his shoulder. Little by little her hand went down his side until it stayed, gently stroking his thigh. He had been lying on his back, rigid with the inner struggle of how to avoid either being surly or in giving in to her furtive advances.

These came as the culmination of anxiety which had been with him all day, in spite of having so much else to do and think about. He had seen her undress as if it was, for them both, a nightly routine and in pretending not to notice, his fear had mounted. Railing inwardly at himself for lacking the courage to remind her at the outset of her undertaking to row in with his celibacy, it had become even harder to push her hand away from his body. And then as it stroked his thigh, his resistance began to collapse as his erection stiffened.

'Oh Tom,' she whispered plaintively. 'Come in and forget all your worries. I know you can and you needn't be afraid any more.'

When his renewed energy was spent, she kissed him and thanked him feelingly, and within minutes he was asleep.

He woke to another kiss from Shirley next morning and had to agree with her that it was the soundest night's sleep he'd had for a long time. But after breakfast, with the cares of the day and the future crowding into his mind, he tried to push aside the implications which the night had engendered. The choice would not have to be made until their cottage was ready to inhabit – or co-habit – with Shirley.

All through the day, except for hurried meals, Tom dealt with his plants whilst Shirley made the house more habitable. 'I want it to be a home you can relax in,' she told him. 'But it will be tomorrow night before it's ready for use, with food in the larder and a good fire to keep out the damp and cold. But while you're indoors, just take that suitcase with your clothes in and leave it at the top of the stairs. I'll deal with it for you later.'

Back in the garden, heeling in his plants, Tom wondered how and where she would deal with his clothes. Until last night he was sure they would be in what he'd expected to be his own bedroom. Now it was as if he had no will of his own and could do no other than let her decide. But she'd better not try to undermine the independence of spirit which had taken years to acquire. It might well be not so bad as he'd feared to give in to her on the sexual side of marriage just now and then for the sake of peace and a measure of harmony. He realised, somewhat dimly, that in the past he had probably taken the sex act too seriously, just as he'd regretted having had no experience of sex and women before he fell in love with Shirley. His then ideals had been shattered, and celibacy appeared to be the only alternative in keeping with his impotence. But he must never allow her to possess him.

Perhaps Shirley had not after all plotted to compromise him into resuming full marital relations. She might have foreseen the opportunity the move to Melthorpe would present and then just let nature – her female nature, take its course. In the sense that women were the more vulnerable and less muscular than men because of child bearing, had struck Tom as being true. Now her attitude was as if she'd seen her mistake and was wanting to make amends for her past shortcomings.

Tom had never probed that period. He had been too absorbed by his own problems both material and mental. The latter were apt to crop up unbidden, but although he had no inkling of their relation to his lack of self-identity, he also lacked the means and ability to sift and sort out the jumble of thoughts which often assailed him. Behind these were what vestiges of ambition he had left, provided he hung on somehow to the now meagre stock of his plants – just a few each of nearly two hundred species and varieties.

Just now, bringing them to a place where he expected no one else would be in the least interested in them, his old ambition was at a very low ebb. Only his love for them remained as a spur. And only his yearning to come to terms with himself remained as another kind of ambition to be pursued as best he could, and he must not, he told himself, allow Shirley to stand in the way, now that a sexual relation with her once more seemed inevitable.

In accepting this, the second night they stayed with her parents in Melthorpe village was much less fraught than the first had been. It was now Friday and on the Saturday morning he was due to confer with his employer as a prelude to regular work on the Monday. In the fading light of that Friday evening he was making sure that none of his plants needed watering when he heard a knock on the front door of the cottage. With a few brisk paces he was in time to see Shirley shaking hands with Anne Potts. 'Pleased to meet you,' Shirley said with a half curtsey.

Anne turned to face him. 'Hallo,' she greeted him with breezy informality. 'We got back from London early and I thought I'd pop along to see if all was well – and in case you needed anything we could help you with.'

'So far as I know –' Tom began, but Shirley took over from him.

'Yes thank you Mrs Potts,' she said, her face aglow with smiles. 'You see, we've stayed two nights with my folks and Mum, she did what shopping we needed today — she always goes on the bus to

Attleborough every Friday — while I stayed to get the house all ready for us. Would you like to come in Mrs Potts?'

'Not this time,' Anne replied. 'I must get back, but I just felt like a short walk to get London air out of my lungs. But I'm glad you're getting settled in and I hope you'll both be happy here in Melthorpe.'

'I'm sure we shall be Mrs Potts,' Shirley confirmed.

Tom still stood by, feeling a little awkward.

Facing him again, Anne said, 'I may see you in the morning as I hear you're coming to discuss the garden with my husband. Thank goodness it's warmer than it was that day you came for the interview, though I didn't see much of you. I probably won't tomorrow either because the major has firm ideas on how he wants the garden to look. Incidentally, he told me you wanted to bring a collection of your own plants, but will you have room for them here as well as your vegetables?'

'That's what's worrying me,' Tom said wryly. 'I've half filled the plot already with a lot more plants to unpack. But there, your husband said it was up to me how I used what garden space goes with the house – and for me the plants have to take priority.'

Three weeks later on a dull Saturday afternoon, Tom wheeled the first barrow load of plants along the lane from his own garden to the rear entrance of the manor. The plot which Gerald had allocated to him was far from ideal. It was close to the potting shed but very little had been grown there as a nearby chestnut tree cast its shadows and spread its roots around. Even some ancient clumps of rhubarb were languishing in the starved soil, now bone dry because no appreciable rain had fallen for three weeks. After the first few days the wind had slewed round to the east, bringing low cloud by day from the North Sea, but clear nights with a touch of frost.

Tom's request had been met with breezy acceptance by Gerald Potts. He had explained that he could only allow him to use a piece of ground well away from the flower garden. It had to be out of sight of the summer visitors on open days lest his flowers tempted people to wander through the kitchen garden to see them. The kitchen garden was out of bounds to the public, and there must be nothing in sight which could detract from the main garden display. Gerald also reminded Tom that in view of the six month trial, he would expect his plants to be removed as soon as possible in the event of his not staying in the job after Michaelmas – the end of the six months period.

Although Tom had guessed that Gerald had deliberately chosen the site as more of a deterrent than a favour, he had no choice but to accept. And he was still smarting from a comment Shirley made when he told her a better place could have been selected which would not have depleted the area for vegetables.

'Well,' she said tartly, 'I s'pose beggars can't be choosers, can they?'

In swallowing what he felt to be a cruel jibe, Tom became more aware that Shirley was herself conscious of a slowly increasing tension between them again.

Chapter Four

Susan was home for the weekend. Gerald had given her a Mini on her twentieth birthday and it only took an hour or so to travel from Cambridge. For her, homecoming was sometimes more of a duty than a pleasure. Not that she lacked affection for her parents, and she felt a sense of gratitude towards Anne for having always encouraged her to develop as an individual and to be self reliant. But she knew Anne herself must have stifled her own independence, Gerald being the type of man he was. Not that he was completely overbearing, but the aura of superiority he had created for himself was like an invisible barricade. Even his generosity towards Susan and Anne was part of it, and although Susan was aware of Anne's constricted way of life, she could neither penetrate her reserve nor express any sympathy. She believed she could see beneath her father's armour, to find there a man less superior than he believed he was. But this insight she had to keep to herself along with a slight twinge of hypocrisy for playing up to his whims and idiosyncrasies as she'd done ever since early childhood.

Another deterrent to frequent homecomings for Susan was that routines never changed. At Melthorpe each of the four seasons brought the same things to be seen or done, and there was but little variation on the people who came to stay or who joined them for tennis or shooting parties. Only last year she had been given permission to have a party of her own – tennis, swimming in the large heated pool of Gerald's design. Having no local friends, a dozen or so undergrads of both sexes came. Gerald made no direct complaint of their lack of respect for his property and restraint in their behaviour, his frowns and silences were enough to warn Susan never to repeat the experiment. And still she could not show herself to be other than a fond, somewhat pampered, but respectful daughter, with a little giggle inside at her own duplicity, and how shocked he'd be if she told him the party had left her no longer a virgin. She would never think of telling her mother either. Anne would, she guessed, merely shrug and smile with some remark about it being entirely her own affair what she did with her body, having explained sex matters to her long ago.

Susan had arrived in time for mid-morning coffee. Soon afterwards Gerald enticed her to take a walk with him round the garden while Anne said she would join them as soon as she could.

'The tulips are just at their best, and the wallflowers of course, but the polyanthus are just going over,' he explained as they walked across the lawn to the laid out garden beyond.

'Did you have a good day last Sunday? It was your first Open Day, wasn't it?' Susan asked.

'It could have been a lot better,' he complained. 'But it was simply due to the weather. Dull and quite cold with drizzle now and then. Even so, over two hundred did turn up, and the produce stall took nearly as much as they did at the gate.'

Susan commiserated suitably and then asked how the new head gardener was shaping.

'So, so,' he replied reservedly. 'He works well enough I suppose, but I fancy his heart's not in it. I don't think he sees the value of my kind of garden and I can't get him to be – well enthusiastic in his manner and what he says. He takes my orders and carries them out, but never says 'That's a good idea' like old Hicks used to say when I suggested some colour combination in bedding out. Of course I insisted on a six month trial and I'm beginning to think he's not for us.'

'Oh dear,' Susan murmured. She could think of nothing else to say that he might be glad to hear, conscious as she was of her own lack of enthusiasm for all these formal beds. She was tempted to be flippant by remarking that the tulips looked like battalions of soldiers standing to attention wearing different coloured busbys, but thought it wiser to refrain. 'Let's go through the greenhouse,' she suggested as they reached the yew hedge screening the kitchen garden. 'It's really quite chilly. What a difference it would make if the sun came out.'

Through the two wall-backed greenhouses they sauntered. In one the Black Hambro grape vines were shading trays in which begonias were sprouting. On all the benches there were plants in trays or pots awaiting the next phase of outdoor bedding. Geraniums, lobelia, salvia, petunias, stocks, echevarias, dahlias and others of Gerald's favourites were there by the hundred. He prided himself in never having to buy bedding plants unless it was some new variety which took his fancy at the Chelsea Show. On the floor were large pots of arum lily now being dried off, along with agapanthus and oleanders destined for the patio between house and lawn. Still more, Susan knew, were in the frames outside, but she had no wish to see the pots and boxes of chrysanthemums and African marigolds which she disliked, and since Anne had not come out to join them she made an excuse to go back to the house and find her.

'I think I'll stay here awhile,' Gerald said, taking up the water can. 'Berkeley's not too good at watering – hurries over it – and there's a few pots in need. See you at lunch, but I have to go and look at a property near Swaffham this afternoon – people only there for the weekend you know.'

'Like you and mum,' Susan called back unthinkingly over her shoulder.

'If you like,' he retorted in the same jocular way. 'But I have a sounder reason for spreading my work load than most and it's only three days out of seven in London.'

'What shall we do?' Anne asked Susan after lunch when Gerald had left.

'I'm easy,' replied Susan. It wasn't swimming weather, nor did a long walk appeal, much less to go to Norwich on a Saturday. She'd seen all she wanted to see of the garden and would be quite content to stay lazily indoors and watch the telly. Then, by degrees, Anne confided that she felt strongly inclined to retain the Webley farm she'd been left under her father's will, for herself. Susan thought it a splendid idea. 'Let's go over there shall we? I'm sure Grandma would be pleased if you told her.'

'All right, so we will in a little while,' Anne said pensively aware of the need to be circumspect. She thought it wiser not to tell Susan how Gerald had given his views recently on the future of the farm. His attitude then had only served to strengthen her own leanings towards taking it over, but she'd now reached the point where it appeared needful to tell her mother, having had Susan's approval. Till now she had kept her thoughts to herself, building up arguments with which to counter opposition, and she couldn't feel entirely certain that her mother would approve either.

'Before we go,' she said casually, 'I'd rather like to take a look at some plants Tom Berkeley has brought. I had to be the one to ask

Gerald to let him have a little plot in the kitchen garden because they wouldn't all cram into what goes with his house.'

On the way she told Susan what little she knew about Tom's past and how she felt rather sorry for him, suspecting that it was his wife who persuaded him to take a post which was not in line with his own gardening ideas.

As they turned through the opening of the high yew hedge they saw Tom was at work on the plot near the chestnut tree, so intent with digging that he hadn't noticed them coming.

'Hard at it Tom?' Anne said.

He paused, resting one foot on his spade. 'Being dry makes it harder – and the tree roots. I hope the major won't think cutting some will damage the tree. Just in case I've made a pile of roots behind the shed there, out of sight.'

'Sensible thing to do,' Anne commented, wishing to avoid any involvement in such an inhospitable site being allocated to him. 'But at least there's a water tap handy,' she added, pointing to a nearby standpipe.

'I'll need it,' he said wryly, resuming his digging.

'Are they the plants you're getting the ground ready for?' Susan asked, indicating the trays piled up on the barrow. 'Can we take a look?'

'Of course,' replied Tom, 'if you're interested.' For the next ten minutes he gave them botanic names and descriptions as he stood the trays down side by side on the ground, scarcely looking at the labels. In between he told them how he'd had to cram them temporarily into the confined space of his cottage garden, knowing they would have to be thinned out before new growth became too advanced. His enquiries for a plot elsewhere in the parish had brought no relief to his anxiety and if, thanks to Anne, the major had agreed to accommodate him, even this dry, half shaded site was better than nothing.

Encouraged by their interest and concern, he found himself talking more freely than with anyone since he came to Melthorpe. Even with the few brief conversations he'd had with Anne over the past few weeks he'd felt somewhat on the defensive and decidedly on edge with Gerald always talking down to him. He also explained that he'd brought only the kinds of plants which would tolerate the chestnut's shade. His plan was to put down a line, cut out a trench against it in which to set the plants, half fill back with soil and then row by row fill it with water from the hosepipe. 'It's what's known as puddling,' he explained. 'When the water's soaked in round the roots, then I push the rest of the dry soil back to leave a tilth on top, and they'll be all right for a week or two before I have to water again overhead if it doesn't rain.'

Anne then said they must leave him to it. When out of earshot, Susan remarked flippantly that Tom was a nut case, but added, 'Not really – I mean he's so devoted, and yet I suspect there's quite an interesting person behind his craggyness. And as a specimen of manhood, he's rather dishy.'

Anne added quietly, 'I can only feel sorry for him.'

Before she could add anything more she was checked by Tom's hastening up behind with, 'Mrs Potts! There's something I've been wanting to ask you, if it isn't presumptuous.' With fingers rustling his tousled, already greying hair, he stood there, somewhat gaunt and lean, his legs shifting uneasily.

'Yes, Tom, what is it?' Anne said, fearing it would be another request to be the go-between.

'I – I hardly like to ask, but would you have a book or two I could borrow? What few I bought I've read again and now I'm feeling sort of starved.'

'Why, of course. I've lots of paperbacks – mostly novels if that's what you'd like. I'll pick some out and put them in the shed if you're not here. Novels okay?'

'I'd rather read serious sorts of books like biographies, historical and even those about – well – what makes people tick, like.'

And when Anne had said she would see what she could find for him and was again out of earshot, Susan reminded her, saying, 'My hunch was right then, there is something behind his craggy exterior. And with human behaviour in my curriculum I'd quite like to know what it is. Maybe I'll bring a book or two next time I come.'

Half an hour later they drove into Dunsford Farm yard and on to the gravel strewn front of the old house. Knowing her mother's preference to be informed in advance of visitors coming, Anne had telephoned. She had also changed into a skirt because of her mother's dislike of women wearing trousers, but Susan had decided to keep on her jeans. Eileen Webley was dressed plainly in black and grey and being quite tall, with almost white hair, these accentuated the rather severe expression she wore.

'I'd begun to wonder if you'd gone for another holiday. It's over a week since you last telephoned.'

'Sorry mother, but it's been rather hectic one way and another, but with Susan home it was a chance not to be missed of us both coming to see you. How are things? You are obviously bearing up very well. I do admire your courage.'

'That goes for me too, Grandma,' Susan chimed in, 'but you have lots of friends and I expect some drop in to keep you from being alone all the time.'

Having made one or two deprecating remarks Eileen said she had a kettle on the boil for tea, and then they must get down to some serious talking. Some vital decisions had to be made and things must not be allowed to drift on. Ten minutes later with tea poured and cake sliced the inevitable question came. But it was not in the form Anne would have expected. Instead, she asked if it was true Gerald would be taking the farm over with his own, and paying her a top rate annual rent.

'As a matter of fact he called in this afternoon on his way to Swaffham on business and said he hoped I would agree when you'd decided this would be the best solution. He said he'd see to it that just the kind of house I wanted would be found wherever I decided to live. It all seemed sensible and reasonable, until he asked me not to tell you he'd called and made the offer. And that's why I'm telling you, Anne. It's your decision and I don't like back door diplomacy, any more than your father did.'

'Thanks for telling me mother,' Anne said, scarcely opening her lips, deciding to let neither of them know how Gerald had broached the subject already in a way that annoyed her. Any lingering indecision had left her now.

'I want to run the farm myself, with advice from you, and of course Ted Fletcher as foreman. He knows what to do and when to do it, and I've not forgotten much of what I knew about farming. And it'll be your choice whether you stay here or wherever. The Will provides for another place for you to live if you don't wish to stay here. That'll be your decision, mother, now you know what mine is.'

Susan, leaning forward with a hand cupped under her chin, her grey eyes wide open, broke in with, 'Well said mother. I think it's a great idea, don't you Grandma? It's the most decisive speech you've made for years. You need an interest of your own after twenty odd years of – well, we won't say second fiddle – it's not very apt.'

Eileen sat wide-eyed and stirred her tea again. 'That's the last thing I would have expected you to do,' she said quietly. 'But won't it upset Gerald and your social life? I mean, life's pretty full as it is, isn't it?'

'Not full enough,' Anne retorted. 'I'm in a rut and now's my chance to get out of it.'

'But what if I decide to live somewhere else? I'd be willing to stay on for a while until it was sold or let to someone else, but not for the rest of my days. I don't see things at all clearly now I must say. I think Gerald's idea was to sell the house separately if he took over the land, and that might be your best plan, if you only want the farm as an interest.'

'I might let the house mother, but I wouldn't want to sell it away from the farm. Who knows what the situation will be in, say, twenty or thirty years' time? There could be another generation in the family wanting to be a farmer. What say you, Susan?'

'I'm saying nothing – about the future I mean. Julian will no doubt inherit Melthorpe and I hope I'm a long way off producing offspring, if ever I do,' she replied gaily.

'But you'll inherit this place,' Anne said with conviction, but surprised at her sudden emergence of positive thinking and decisive manner. It was like a new and exciting sensation inside herself that was bubbling up to give it expression. 'Until now,' she added thoughtfully, 'I hadn't anything worth making a will for, but now I have. In case I get run over by a bus, I'll go and see a solicitor in Attleborough next time I go shopping, so there!'

Then she began to laugh. That was when Susan came across to her and gave her a kiss and a hug, which made her want to change from laughing to weeping. A glance at her mother calmed her, for Eileen sat bolt upright with a very puzzled expression on her austere features. Then on sudden impulse Anne went across to put one arm around her mother's rigid back and kissed the top of her forehead. 'Bear with me, mother,' she whispered. 'I've had a lot on my mind lately, trying to come up with the right answer. Suddenly it came, and I felt such a relief that I lost control. But I want you to feel free to do just what you wish. I know losing Dad as well as Brian has knocked the bottom out of your world and it must come hard to face up to your own future, but never forget that I'll not be happy until I know you are as content as can be in your situation.'

The sun was peeping through little breaks here and there in the low, grey westbound clouds. Anne and Susan took a short walk round the spick and span farm buildings, past the shed in which clean tractors and machinery were parked for the weekend, and leaned over the gate where the small herd of Friesians were contentedly grazing. To the left of the meadow the round-towered church was half hidden by trees, as was the course of the little river on the far side.

'Almost idyllic,' Susan murmured, 'and I'm glad it's yours to carry on Grandpa's management of it. You will – now that you've taken yourself in hand and made your mind up to be yourself. Will you tell Gerald when we get back?'

It was the first time she'd used his first name in Anne's hearing and it made her blink. It had always been 'Daddy', but if she wished now to make another break from childhood when she thought fit, then it was up to her, though she wasn't likely to use 'Gerald' to his face.

'It would be best not to,' Anne replied. 'If he doesn't refer to his calling in here on his way to Swaffham, I'll just say we came to cheer mother up a little. It'll come out soon enough and I don't want anything to spoil your weekend. We'll let sleeping dogs lie, eh?'

Back at Melthorpe they found Gerald in the lounge watching television. He said he'd found the note telling him where they'd gone and having added that he was feeling peckish it gave Anne the idea of getting a quick meal ready with Susan's help. Feeling replete with ham and scrambled eggs, Gerald was in a relaxed mood as he went to his study, excusing himself. Pausing as he left the table, he raised his eyebrows with a crafty smile. 'I don't reckon to talk shop at home, but I can tell you that I spent three hours this afternoon with a belted earl who's having to sell his ancestral estate. Just a matter of seven thousand acres including two villages as well as his stately mansion. All I need to do is to work out some figures and I fancy by this time next week it'll be in the bag. Not a word to anyone, mind you. Ah! Thanks Anne, I'll take my coffee and cognac with me. I'll be back in time for the news.'

'There goes a very satisfied man,' Susan said flippantly when he closed his study door.

'I'm afraid his mood will be very different when he knows I'm taking over the farm,' Anne murmured as she poured out their own coffee. 'It's very odd,' she added thoughtfully, 'here am I suddenly being a schemer, practising the same kind of diplomacy as your father. But now I'm a wee bit afraid I might wilt when the time comes, as it must very soon, and I won't have you to back me up then, will I?'

'You won't get cold feet if you keep reminding yourself of the dismal alternative. If you don't stand up to him now, you never will.'

Anne gave her a grateful smile. 'Bless you, Susan.'

It was Susan who suggested now would be a propitious time to look for a few books for Tom Berkeley, with no risk of Gerald asking questions. It had never been one of his ambitions to collect books as a library for prestige purposes. His study contained all he needed in his profession and Anne's own accumulation was on shelves and even in cupboards in her dressing room. Most of them were paperback novels she'd acquired for holidays rather than for reading at home. She told Susan that more still were in their London house because there she had more time on her hands.

'Here's one!' Susan exclaimed. 'It's the one I got for you, remember? The Spirit of the Valley, by Sukie Colegrave. This'll make him blink when he reads it.'

Anne found Elaine Morgan's Descent of Woman and Trevelyan's English Social History. 'These'll last him a week or two,' she chuckled.

When Rogue Herries, also in paperback was found, they agreed it was enough, and Susan offered to see they were wrapped and left next day in the potting shed with a reminder that she must bring one or two of her own next time she came.

'And it won't be long. I'll want to know most of all how you make out mother. After all, I've a vested interest now, haven't I?'

As they went downstairs the telephone rang, but only once, which meant Gerald had answered it.

Chapter Five

The contrast between conversing with Anne and Susan and with Shirley made a forcible impact on Tom. It was not a case of them having similar interests to himself, but simply that they made him feel at ease. He decided not to tell Shirley of the encounter, fearing it might be just a one-off occurrence. But there was a vast difference between their attitude towards him and that of Gerald, whose voice and manner made even a discussion on ways and means sound like a military briefing.

He found the little parcel of books when he went on Sunday to do the watering for which he was responsible. But his excitement at seeing their titles was quickly offset by thoughts of Shirley. Either he would have to tell a white lie about their origin, or keep them secret. It wouldn't work. He'd got to be open and just say it was an offer of a loan and use the occasion to remind her of her failure to select his kind of book from the mobile library. 'Hell!' he said inwardly, 'why should it be so difficult to indulge in my own harmless pursuits?' What right had Shirley of all people to make him feel guilty again? But those questions stayed with him unanswered until he went home.

'What's in that parcel?' was Shirley's first question.

'Books.'

'Where from?' she persisted.

Then he told her that Anne and Susan had stopped to talk and had asked if he ever read anything but gardening books. This, he thought, was a neat way out, until Shirley began to probe further.

At first Tom wanted to protest at what he saw as an inquisition, but the right words would not come and he let her carry on as he washed at the kitchen sink. Then, wiping his face on the roller towel, he faced her, his deep-set eyes glinting. 'Have you finished?' he asked firmly.

Shirley took up the books from the kitchen table and tossed them on to the nearby dresser disdainfully. 'No, I haven't! And I tell you straight, if you're going back to your old ways which drove us apart, then I'm going to get a job. Daphne told me a new hotel just outside Attleborough on the A11 is looking for experienced staff and I'm going to apply. The car is still mine, don't forget, and you don't need it anyway. I'm sure Mrs Potts would lend you hers if you did.'

It was the old Shirley back again, Tom reflected, but it was somehow easier now to absorb her complaints. Her hold over him, he now found, was weakened, making it quite easy to come out with, 'That's okay by me Shirley. And I'll be sleeping in the other room from now on.' It was all he needed to say to ease the weight on his mind. Shirley shot a wide-eyed glance of surprise and the meal of sausage and mash she had ready was eaten in almost total silence.

Trevor, the junior of his two young helpers was quick to notice a change in Tom next morning. Both he and Michael showed considerable interest in the now completed rows of his plants he'd dug in and watered. Tom briefly pointed out a few, explaining what they would look like when they flowered.

'No wonder you looked so worried the last week or two, with all that lot takin' harm in this dry weather.'

'The forecast says rain's coming before night,' Michael put in.

Tom told them it was time to get stuck into earthing up the early potatoes, while he did the watering as usual. Then, inside the lean-to greenhouses he found Gerald.

'Ah! – Berkeley! I was about to come and find you. I saw your bed of plants last evening and reckoned you must have been pretty lavish with the water.'

'It was very dry there sir,' Tom replied, 'but I never reckon to waste water.'

'Maybe not, but if restrictions have to come because of the drought, my garden takes priority, don't forget, and that includes the lawn. I can't have that going brown. I hear rain may be coming tonight, so I'll leave it till morning before I go to London to map out the work while I'm away. The seasonal routine I've worked out has to be on a pretty strict timetable. I don't wish my son, who's coming next weekend, to tell me the garden is looking less cared for than when Hicks was in charge. Master Julian had a soft spot for him, and so did I for that matter – he was so used to my routine that he didn't need to be told what to do and just when to do it. It would have done you good to have had a season with him before taking over.'

Tom felt the sting behind Gerald's remarks. It was as if his work so far fell short of his employer's expectations, yet all he could say was, 'I'll do my very best sir.' He was not to know that Gerald had chosen his words with an end in view.

That end was explained more fully not long after Julian arrived a few days later in his MG from Oxford. Julian had but a superficial interest in the garden, but it was his father's habit to make this the first excursion round the estate. Now, close to the end of his university career, Julian was much more interested in the farm, hearing of his father's activities as a property expert with Wroxley, Ross and Partners. Company and estate law had been his bent at Brazenose and with Gerald's full backing he was due to widen his knowledge of estate management and agriculture before coming into the firm by a course at Cirencester College.

Julian, rising twenty-three, was an inch taller than his father but less heavily built. Gerald's pride in having fathered such an upstanding specimen of manhood was just beginning to be offset by a little fear that Julian's ascent in the professional ladder might be more rapid than his own had been. He was not disposed to step aside for him. Not for a long time. But neither could he very well do other than encourage him and support his ambitions. There were no certainties in life he'd reflected, and if his own life ended prematurely, it would be comforting to think his son would be fully competent to make the best of what he would inherit.

When told that Tom Berkeley would not be staying on, Julian remarked that the six-month trial period had been a wise precaution on Gerald's part. But he showed little or no concern, except to agree on the distinctive merits of his pattern of gardening, and that it shouldn't be hard to find a new gardener with the right ideas.

'Lately,' Gerald mused, 'I've come to wish your mother had them too. She'd prefer the modern higgledy-piggledy form of gardening, which is what I fancy Berkeley hoped I would adopt.' They were standing close to Tom's plot. Julian bent down to read the name on the nearest label. 'Cimicifuga japonica acerina – I s'pose that means something to some people, but not to me. Does it to you?'

'Absolutely nothing,' Gerald snorted.

'Talking of mother,' Julian went on, to bring an abrupt end to the subject, 'your last letter said you hoped she'd let Grandpa's farm to you, but was dithering about making up her mind. Has she decided yet?'

'No, and I haven't the heart to push her. She's disinclined to discuss it with me and won't be drawn.'

'Hm!' Julian grunted. 'Do you think I should try while I'm here? I can see it's becoming a worry for you. You need to know, don't you?'

'I'd rather you didn't, Julian. She might even guess that I'd put you up to it. I don't like it but I'll just have to be patient,' Gerald said, thinking it would also be wise not to tell him he'd had a chat about it with his grandmother. Gerald's anxiety over the future of Dunsford Farm was replaced next day by much deeper misgivings.

The sun had come through after another welcome rain early that Saturday morning. Gerald and Julian had been all round the Home Farm together and with lunch over Gerald said he felt the need for a rest with feet up in his study. 'Give me half an hour, and I'll be ready for anything,' he said breezily as he made for his study.

For reasons of her own Anne was glad she'd not needed to prompt him to take a rest. 'If you've nothing better to do Julian,' she suggested, 'come and keep me company. I'll just stuff the plates in the dishwasher if you'll bring the left-overs.'

In the sunlit lounge, Anne said calmly that time should be allowed to visit Dunsford Farm and her mother. 'I'd quite like to take a walk round the fields,' she added casually. 'You see, I've decided to be a farmer and run it myself. Does that surprise you Julian?'

The expression on his very masculine features at once showed surprise. 'It certainly does. But why, for goodness sake?'

'Why? Well, dear, it's my farm now and I mean to make sure it's carried on as Grandpa would have wished.'

'But mother,' Julian persisted, 'I don't understand. I mean, you're telling me before you've told father. He's been hoping you'd let it to go in with his farm, and that made sense to me. Small farms aren't economic these days.'

'Grandpa made a fair living from it and I think I still know enough about farming to do the same, with Ted Fletcher's help as foreman. Besides, and I may as well be frank with you, I feel the need for an interest and involvement of my own now that you and Susan are adults making your own way.'

Julian, sitting tensed and bolt upright in his chair, still looked incredulous and puzzled. 'But I still don't understand. Even if I can see your point of view, I can't see it working out. For one thing farming is scarcely ever a job women take to. Not that you need to milk cows and feed pigs, or drive a tractor.'

'I used to drive one sometimes, before I married,' Anne smiled.

'But it's the effect it will have on father that bothers me most. You haven't told him. But my guess is that you know he'll be upset, and rightly, because it'll probably disrupt his – his ordered way of life, and at his age he'll not take kindly to a radical change.'

Anne's face broke into a forced smile. 'It needn't be radical. I've no wish to upset him. But I've deferred to him and fallen in with his way of life for twenty odd years and now there's a chance to be myself, independently, I've decided to take it. I can still play my full part here and I won't need to be at Dunsford every day.'

'I still don't like it mother,' Julian said after a brief silence. 'Apart from the merging of the two farms making more economic sense, I'm afraid you'll begin to find the mid-week days in London irksome.'

'They are already Julian,' Anne exclaimed, 'and have been for quite a long time. I'd much rather stay behind, but I've put up with going out of loyalty. And I have been loyal Julian, too much so perhaps, to allow me to become a person in my own right. Or do you think like your father seems to, that I should be content with being more like a shadow or reflection of another's personality because I'm only his wife?' Anne suddenly realised she was close to tears because she was uttering clearly for the first time what before had been jumbled, taunting thoughts.

Julian, quite oblivious to her rising emotion, lit a cigarette as he began to fidget and finger with his college necktie. 'You'll have to tell him now,' he warned. 'But what about Susan? – not that she's much concerned. And there's Grandma, she will be wanting to know too.'

'I told them both last week while your father was visiting some earl who wants to sell his estate. Grandma's not against the idea and Susan's all in favour. And that was before I told her the farm would be left to her just as this place will be left to you. As for telling your father, I'd rather you did so please. That's one reason why I've told you first, because you wouldn't want to be either witness or judge of the outcome, and I'll still have plenty to face up to afterwards. I'm off to Dunsford Farm now. He's got to be told before I come back Julian, because I can't be sure of keeping my emotions under control if I have to break it to him.'

Anne's Volvo was speeding along the short drive to the road just as Gerald entered the lounge where Julian was mentally struggling with words. His resentment at being left to break the news was having to be pushed aside because there was no alternative course open to him. He told himself that he must be terse and put Anne's case as fairly as he could, even if his sympathies were already more for Gerald. And also to be fair he must show at least some of the sympathy his father would expect from him, if only because his own ambitions depended on a reasonably close intimacy with him.

'Where's your mother?' Gerald asked, gazing round the room as if she might be hiding herself somewhere.

'She's gone to Dunsford – just this minute left.'

'The devil she has. She might have asked us if we wanted to go along with her, if only to cheer the old lady up. She's taken it pretty hard – her only son and her husband gone inside three years. Besides, it might have given us the chance to find out what's to become of the farm. I'd dearly like to know.'

'I can tell you,' Julian said wryly.

Anne spent an uneasy hour with her mother before she decided she must take a walk on her own. Although her mother Eileen was still favourably inclined, having come to believe that Anne would strive to keep up to her father's high standards of farming, she'd had more misgivings over the effect it would have on Gerald. She had held him in high esteem from the first and saw nothing but the advantages that would come to Anne as his wife.

Having taken the first prodigious step, Anne became more conscious that it would soon have to be followed by another. Gerald, as she imagined what effect Julian's information would have on him, would quickly pounce on the likelihood of her opting out of at least some of the mid-week stays in London. She was in fact steeling herself to resolve never to do so again as the surest way of asserting her independence.

With her head almost choc-a-bloc with pros and cons, Anne let herself through the gate into the home meadow, freshly green from recent rains. The sun shone warmly and birds were singing as she made for the footpath which crossed the fourteen acres. It was a public one leading from the churchyard to save almost a mile for those who walked to Baldisham, the next village upstream of the little river. This was spanned by a decrepit foot bridge which no authority kept in repair because scarcely anyone used the footpath. Taking deep breaths Anne strode across the meadow under the watchful eyes of cows, and on gaining the path, made for the bridge half hidden by willows and alders which marked the course of the stream. Beyond was a field of sugar beet and she had to remind herself that it too belonged to her.

Deciding to go no further, but to linger awhile on the bridge, she wondered if the shaky structure would stand her weight. Having crossed over, casting a look at the young beet plants reviving after the rain and the vestigial path between them and the river, she decided to sit down on the bridge planks and dangle her legs. She remembered seeing a flood which came almost up to the planks, but now the water was lower and clearer, so clear that she could see gently waving weeds and little fish – gudgeon, on the gravelly bottom, and dace nearer the surface. The stream was only four or five yards wide and no more than two feet deep. Slowly a feeling of peace came over her with memories of girlhood pleasures.

Twenty-five or more years ago, the first thing she would do on a warm day would be to slip off her shoes and let her feet dangle in the water. But now she was wearing tights. As she struggled fumblingly to pull them off from beneath her tweed skirt, sheer emotion began to boil over in sobs. Laying the tights aside she sat down again, holding on to the handrail and let her feet into the surprisingly cold water. Then she let the tears come – tears of relief, of an intense joy, knowing she was back to where her roots belonged. Her parents had never shown her the consideration they had afforded to Brian, three years her senior. It was hard sometimes to accept the difference and sometimes it made her feel angry and rebellious. But now all those feelings had gone.

Wiping her eyes with her tights and kicking her toes noisily in the water like she used to do, she did not hear the footsteps approaching from behind the trees on the pathway coming from Baldisham until they sounded on the planks of the bridge.

'I beg your pardon!' came just as she slewed round in fright.

She struggled to hastily expose less of her plump thighs whilst screwing up her tights and clumsily trying to stand upright.

'I'm so sorry to disturb you,' the voice persisted. 'I could not have passed over without doing so.'

Embarrassed and blushing uncomfortably, Anne at last stood up clutching her tights behind her back, to face a tall man probably a little younger than herself, carrying a small suitcase and wearing a dog collar. His open face, despite a short beard, displayed concern and embarrassment. Then slowly he began to smile.

'Having so rudely disturbed you,' he said, 'I'd better introduce myself. I'm Peter Hemming, the new vicar of Dunsford and two other parishes thrown in – Baldisham included, where I've just been officiating at a funeral. And you?'

'I'm Anne Potts from Melthorpe, and this was my father's farm.' She took his proferred handshake.

'People have told me about him, with much respect. I briefly met your mother at church last Sunday and intended to visit her very soon. I'm having to fend more or less for myself at the vicarage – but not for long I hope, though there are problems.

'You see, I had several years in the Army before deciding to take Orders – become a parson, I mean. Now after three years as a curate, I fell for a country living as did my fiancée. But I couldn't let her join me as a wife in Dunsford vicarage because it's too large and in need of repair. So the powers that be have decided to sell it and build a smaller house. But from what I hear, it will take a year or two, what with Ecclesiastic red tape and the Planning Authority. So I'm stuck and we're both getting very impatient. Claire's still living in Nottingham where I first met her, and we can only meet once in a while.'

Anne sympathised as best she could as they walked back to Dunsford.

They reached the point where Anne had joined the path. But instead of leaving him to continue on towards the church and nearby vicarage, she paused and faced him. 'Listen,' she said, 'an idea has just occurred to me. If it works out as I believe it will, it might appeal to you. No harm in telling you straight away, but my mother's living alone in the farmhouse and hasn't decided yet what to do, whether to stay alone, or with a companion help, or move into a smaller house somewhere which I'd have to provide under my father's will. I'm not going to hurry her in making up her mind. She might well prefer a married couple sharing the house with her. Now, if she responds to my gentle hints, would the idea appeal to you Mr Hemming?'

'You can bet it would Mrs Potts, and I know I can speak for Claire too, without having to put it to her. It would be like a gift from heaven.'

Chapter Six

On two counts another visit to Lord Ramsdale's estate came by way of relief to Gerald after a distressing week. It would take his mind off the anger he felt inwardly and the hurt he showed outwardly at Anne's defection – if only for a time. To clinch the deal with the earl would be much to his credit and confirm the unanimous decision of the board of Wroxley, Ross and Partners to elect him as chairman. Yet even this deserved honour would be marred by Anne's sudden lapse and defiance. A celebration party in London would be in order; but he couldn't now rely on her to play her part as hostess. And as he drove towards Marlington Hall, he found such thoughts impinging on the need to keep a clear head for the most prestigious sale he'd ever had proferred.

Gerald's reception in front of the imposing eighteenth century mansion was not a case of being let in by a footman, but by a gruff, 'Morning Potts!' from a youngish man dressed scruffily in sweater and jeans as he stepped out of his Jaguar.

'Lunch won't be ready, my sister says, for another half an hour so I suggest we take a look round the outbuildings at the back. They're adaptable and shouldn't be undervalued as potential conversion.'

Before their first meeting a week ago, Gerald had found out what he could from Burke's Peerage. The Sporles were originally a Norfolk family but their title came from Henry VIII when the first earl was living in Yorkshire. Marlington Hall was built as the seventh earl added to an estate he'd acquired by a judicious marriage. Now, John Sporle had become heir when the 12th earl died childless. His younger brother had emigrated to New Zealand in the 1930s and had died there two years before with John thus becoming the 13th Earl. 'Unlucky thirteenth,' John had joked to Gerald on his first visit. This brought a diplomatic comment from Gerald to the effect that the estate was worth far more now than would have been the case even five years ago.

'I'll admit,' he added, 'that your tenant farmers cannot be turned out if they don't want to become owners, but they are prosperous grain producers and can afford to buy at close to market prices rather than have investing landlords, such as pension fund holders, who they know will put up their rents. But I wouldn't be surprised if we get an offer from one of the big corporations.'

'I don't give a damn who buys the estate so long as I get the money to take back to New Zealand where I can re-invest it. I intend to get back to my wife and family just as soon as I can. But what about the two villages? Most of the houses are on the estate and the occupants will have to dub up or get out, won't they? Or are British laws another hindrance?'

Gerald explained how tenant law stood, adding that the price of houses had likewise rocketed with the demand for country weekend or holiday property from the urban wealthy. John Sporle was keen to have an estimate of the total value of the property and to know how much would be left after estate death duty had been paid. It was these figures that Gerald had been working out in his study when Anne and Susan were looking out books for Tom Berkeley.

What Gerald did not know until this second visit to Marlington Hall was that the earl had a sister, much less that she would be cooking lunch for them. He'd expected it would be taken in one of the smaller ground floor rooms, but instead John Sporle led the way down some steps to the kitchens. 'Charlotte is hanging on to her title, even if she is divorced,' he whispered in advance of introducing her as Lady Norton. It was far from being an aristocratic meal but the chops were well cooked and garnished tastefully. Charlotte was slim to the point of being sleek, with dark hair pulled back from her high forehead, exposing her ears, each dangling with a large jewelled pendant. Quite a striking woman, Gerald reflected, with no lack of poise and easy conversation. Charlotte was more familiar than John with the mansion itself, having stayed there often with her uncle since she remained in England after Roedean and Lady Margaret Hall for her education. She did not hide her regret that John had decided to sell out rather than take on the family heritage. John had told Gerald already that the contents of the house were hers, but because the whole property was his to dispose of, she had virtually no alternative than to have them sold by auction. Many of the most valuable pictures and objets d'art had, however, been sold to pay the previous earl's liability for death duties.

'I'll have you know Mr Potts,' Charlotte declared, 'that it was I who suggested your firm to handle the sale of the estate.' She smiled in a way that made Gerald wonder if she expected an unofficial commission on that account, until she added, 'Of the discreet enquiries I made for John, it must please you to know that Wroxley, Ross came out tops.'

'And I'm due to become Chairman of the Board next week,' he chuckled in a confident tone.

'Good for you,' Charlotte smiled. 'You must deserve it. Who would you recommend me to go to, to auction the contents, Simpsons or Critchleys? They're the experts, aren't they?'

'You can take your pick. They're both equally reliable.'

Gerald decided there was no urgent need to get back to Melthorpe when John asked if he was willing to stay on to tie up every possible loose end, even to fixing dates and how widespread the advertising should be. Over tea and scones Gerald asked where Charlotte was living.

'Oh, here and there. Here, whenever John needs me to housekeep. Not that I mind, because the place has a kind of hold over me, which I know has to give way. When it's all over and John goes back, then I'll be looking for a home of my own, probably London. I envy you men having roots which refuse to be pulled out. I really do. It must have cost my father a hell of a lot to pull his roots up when he saw there was no future for him here as the second son. But now, as you see, John's got his roots deep in New Zealand and he can't bring himself to yank them out to come back here for good. Anyway, I s'pose he's lost touch with the past and the stuff that hereditary earls are made of.'

'Come off it Lottie,' John commented with a grin. 'I've had this all out with you more than once since I inherited. It's inevitable that such places as this will have to be broken up as estates, what with death duties and the radical changes in economics and politics. Why should the privilege they confer be carried on generation after generation, whether the holder's a crank or a crook, or just a parasite. And another thing –.'

Bridling quickly, Charlotte broke in with, 'John Sporle! That's rubbish! Neither Uncle Arthur nor his father were anything but good landlords who cared and upheld the best traditions. You're just being bloody-minded, and you know it.'

John laughed as if he had been deliberately provocative and then asked Gerald if he had any personal views on the subject apart from professional interest.

'I can't help feeling a bit sad to see long established estates being broken up because of modern pressures,' he replied thoughtfully. 'But,' he added seeing the need to be diplomatic, 'even if my business is to assist owners who have decided the end has come, there is another important aspect to it.'

'What's that?' Charlotte queried.

'Estate management. It's a separate and very important department of Wroxley, Ross and Partners. Some owners make use of our expertise by asking us to take over. We appoint competent estate managers and supervisors whose job it is to see that an estate is run efficiently and have accounts audited to ensure it yields the best possible return on the capital value – and to keep up the kind of traditions desired by the owner. We take care of tenancies and see that all tenant farmers abide by the rules of good husbandry. We even take on forestry where woodlands are concerned. It's a good system and it works. You'd be surprised if you knew the names of some of the estates we manage.'

Gerald had spent over six hours at Marlington Hall and was feeling the better for it as he drove quite slowly along the tree-lined drive to the public road. Then as reflections on his visit veered towards Melthorpe and his personal problems, his anger against Anne was giving way to a more rational view. The hurt feeling was if anything more intense but he was just beginning to realise that anger could but produce negative results. She had as it were slapped him on both cheeks, deciding not to let him run her parental farm, followed – as a result of his annoyance – by refusing to go on the next mid-week stay in London.

'You'll be sorry for this!' he'd almost snarled, and it was then she had walked sedately out of his study and gently closed the door. Now he had to admit to himself, she had come through the encounter without loss of dignity. He would have expected her to fall the victim of her own emotions, but she'd controlled them and behaved much as he would have done in a reversed situation. But emotions were a female weakness and if he couldn't play on them by showing anger, then he must find another way to break her obstinate resistance. Till now he'd thought he knew her inside and out, seeing and understanding her faults and weaknesses with kindly tolerance, boosting her ego with compliments and gifts.

There should be no distractions from his mounting determination to break her resistance in time to have her meekly with him as usual on Tuesday morning en route for London.

He entered by the back door of the house and was met by the smell of garlic. And there at the kitchen Aga was Anne chatting to a man standing beside her.

'You're just in time,' Anne greeted him easily, 'I'm doing enough Spaghetti Bolognese for three. And this is Peter Hemming, the new vicar. Poor man, he's having to more or less fend for himself in that awful old vicarage, so I asked him to join us.'

With no alternative but to respond to Peter's proferred hand, Gerald's thoughts began to whirl as Peter smilingly explained that he'd made a courtesy call. 'The Induction was on a Wednesday evening three weeks ago, but you didn't miss much of a ceremony, nor was the Bishop in top form. And I'm not going to induce you into becoming regular churchgoers, much as it would please me to see you there sometimes. My first duty is to make what friends I can in my three parishes.'

Neither Gerald nor Anne had attended church more than two or three times a year, though they were Anglicans. Each had their own reasons for so seldom using the front pew below the pulpit which was reserved for the manor. Gerald took the view that they should at least show an example to the villagers once in a while. But Anne, finding the service archaic and out of keeping with her secret but vague ideas and beliefs, had made the effort in deference to her mother.

Over the meal, Anne told Gerald that in all probability Peter and his wife would be sharing Dunsford farmhouse with her mother. It came out as if had cropped up earlier that evening, Peter having agreed to say nothing of their encounter on the footbridge a week ago.

'I take it your mother's agreeable?' Gerald asked, more casually than he felt, with his resolves having to be shelved.

'Well, you know mother,' Anne explained with tongue in cheek. 'She always likes to consider, but after a few questions over the phone had been answered satisfactorily, she's delighted at the prospect.'

'So am I,' Peter said, 'and I can't tell you how grateful I am.

'And now,' Anne hinted, 'I hope you'll be able to sleep better Mr Hemming for what little we've been able to do for you this evening.'

'Of course. I must be off,' he exclaimed, looking at his watch and rising briskly from his chair.

Gerald decided to wait until the next evening before confronting Anne. When she returned from Dunsford Gerald gave her a sideways look and a smile. 'So that's another lame dog you've helped,' he said, and then added with low voiced intensity, 'but don't you realise how you've maimed me? It beggars me when I think how callous and cruel you've been and I've racked my brains trying to think what I've done to deserve it. What shocks and distresses me is the cold, calculating way you've behaved, as if I'd been your worst enemy instead of your husband who's been faithful and devoted to you. How could you do this to me Anne?'

'I did what I had to do, Gerald,' she said with more firmness than she felt, fully conscious that his new approach was likely to be more deadly than anything she'd had to endure following Julian's disclosure. His accusation of cruelty stabbed her for all her knowing that he was now using a more subtle ploy. She could feel her emotions clambering to emerge but fought them back, a voice inside telling her to say as little as possible.

'If I could have avoided hurting you, I would, but there was no other way.'

'But you're hurting others too. Can't you see that Julian and Susan will see your refusal to go with me any more to London as a threat to family unity? And how on earth am I to explain it to all the people there? It wouldn't have been so devastating if you'd opted out just now and then, gradually. And to think I'd planned a special celebration for being elected Chairman of the Board! But there, I expect you're gloating inside because that's another body blow at me you're able to inflict.'

'I'm sorry Gerald,' Anne said softly. 'It took me a long time to decide I must be more independent, but having done so I know it would be fatal to give in – even partially. There is no room for compromise that I can see.'

'There's none so blind as those that won't see,' Gerald slung out in a desperate tone of voice. 'But believe you me, if you're not willing to make an effort to compromise, you'll come to regret it with as much or more suffering than you're causing me now. To turn on me as you've done after nearly twenty-five years together will have lots of unpleasant repercussions you've never thought of.'

'I'll have to take what comes, Gerald. We all have to accept the outcome of decisions we make, whether we like it or not – don't we?'

'But you've never told me the real reason for making such a dreadful drastic decision – as if loyalty was of no account. Or as if I'd treated you badly. Can't you tell me that now, Anne?'

She stood up from her chair and looked down at him. 'I made my decision with only one thing in mind Gerald. Forget what you think I owe you, because it's just a debt I owe to myself in order to become myself and not just a reflection of you.'

Chapter Seven

The second public opening of Melthorpe Manor Gardens was in June, with the rose beds as the main attraction. Soon after acquiring the property, Gerald had done away with the two rectangular rose beds just in front of the house. There they made a division between the gravelled frontage and the large lawn beyond. The contents were old and gnarled, neglected and gappy. Grass turves were laid in place of roses and three larger beds were made for them on the far side of the lawn in a curving formation. He then decided that the view from the house should sweep over the sward towards them as a floral barrier to the many box-edged formal beds beyond. He therefore had new beds backed by a pergola for climbing pillar roses with blue clematis to add a harmonising colour with whites, pinks and reds. It was still a source of pride to him.

On the second Open Sunday of the year, the bedding plants of geraniums, begonias, stocks and marigolds had replaced the tulips and wallflowers of the spring display, and were just coming into flower. They would, he believed, hold people's gaze away from the still green dahlias and early chrysanthemums in more rear positions, which would ensure continuity right through to the last opening in September. It had been an extra concern this year because Hicks had gone and Berkeley was having to be told what to plant where, although he seemed to know when. Gerald still had not told him that he must leave. Anne had said no more in Tom's favour, nor had they been together so far as he knew more than a few minutes at a time. But such were his deep down feelings towards Anne that he was more than ready to override any suggestion that Tom was too good a gardener to dispense with.

That Sunday began sunny and warm, with hopes, Gerald believed, of making good the lack of support in the spring opening in early May, when it was wet. Long trestle tables in the courtyard at the rear of the house held an array of bedding plants and the old coach house was ready for teas and light refreshments under Anne's charge as usual. There was a table holding mainly paperback books for sale at twenty pence each, which had been brought back from the London home since Anne agreed that she had no further interest in them.

Tom Berkeley's offer to help on the plant stall had been accepted, leaving Gerald to show little groups of visitors around, which he did with gusto, carrying his long stick. Although there was scarcely a weed to uproot, this was useful as a pointer when he needed to draw the attention of a visitor to a variety he knew by name. Gerald reckoned that labels detracted from the beauty of flowers and were unnecessary in his garden.

To open his garden for some good cause was an unalloyed pleasure for Gerald. It was not only pride that was rightly his as being its owner and its inspiration, which all visitors seemed to respect. Some visitors who guessed him to be the owner, shot him respectful glances with a swift salute to their foreheads. Others sidled up to congratulate him on the garden's perfections, and he could answer even the most ignorantly based questions with benevolent ease. The pleasure it was to him had encouraged him to insert larger and more frequent advertisements in the press.

It was a good way of giving more money to charity which otherwise the tax man would grab. And the benign feeling which Open Sundays gave him came as some compensation for Anne's defection.

A frequent question visitors asked was how many helpers he employed. To this he would reply that apart from himself there were only three with the inference that his was the greater commitment. It was wise, he believed, to play down the costs. No one else need or should know that most garden expenses were added to those of the farm and Trevor and Michael were very occasionally put on to farm work when extra help was required. To Gerald it was an almost legitimate means of reducing tax liability, since it was so widely practised. And very gratifying it was to think that in real terms the upkeep of the garden cost him very little indeed.

When it came to advertising for a new head gardener, he hoped it would produce a much better selection than the few who had responded to the last one.

Anne might have won the first round by refusing to go to London with him on the previous Tuesday, but it was, to his mind, only the first round. He had gone to the flat in the house he had now purchased and apart from getting his own breakfast, had taken other meals in a restaurant close to his firm's office. A daily, instead of a twice weekly, domestic help might have to be employed, but if Anne's obstinacy continued he might begin to consider having a housekeeper there all the time, leaving Anne to ponder more deeply on what that might imply. He had lost interest in sex over the past few years and the last time he went to Anne's bedroom was at Christmas. He was not made as welcome as in his whisky-induced ardour he had a right to expect, and when back in his own bedroom had reflected that it had not been worth the mental and physical effort involved. But now after six months abstinence it could well be that a slimmer and perhaps younger woman than Anne in the next bedroom of his flat could arouse him. No one could possibly blame him, least of all Anne. But, as he so often said to himself, he must never let Anne think she had got away with what she had done to him.

Anne herself had no such illusions. She felt quite content in having gained an important victory. It had never been her intention to achieve more than this measure of freedom and independence and the relief of being able to spend the mid-week days at Melthorpe and Dunsford as she chose was even greater than she'd expected. There was joy even in taking over the accounts and in tending the farmhouse garden. She carried on with her usual chores at Melthorpe, made much simpler whilst Gerald was away in London, freed as she was from anticipating his needs and not hearing the sound of his dominating voice.

For many years past, a three-roomed wing of the manor had been occupied by husband and wife service tenants for security during their absence. Anne therefore had no qualms in being alone at night in the main part of the house. By day, with one or two of the workers' wives going about their duties, Anne decided to spend very little time in the manor garden when Gerald was in residence. If she were seen chatting with Tom Berkeley it could cause trouble that must be avoided. Apart from that, her sense of duty, as well as her wish to give no cause for offence, were still strong. She had seen no real disloyalty in standing up for what were her vital, personal rights, but no one else must have just cause to believe she had disrupted family unity.

As for Tom, she was feeling increasing sympathy for him because he had still not been told he would have to find another job, nor dare she plead his cause with Gerald in the present climate. Tom had in fact lost some of the careworn looks so noticeable only a few weeks ago as if he too had overcome some personal anxieties or frustrations. His capacity for work was still an astonishment to her, as if he knew he was under threat of dismissal if he were to slack off. She wished heartily that she could have told him of Gerald's intentions, if only to work less hard and for no more hours per week than he need, and to give him more time to find another post. As for his plot with its rows of plants, she noticed they were sometimes flagging for lack of moisture. Mentioning this one day, Tom explained that the major had told him to use no more water for them than was absolutely necessary, and this was the reason. 'I don't expect them to grow much,' he told Anne, 'but I'll make sure they don't die for lack of water. The rest of them at home are quite flourishing, but neither them nor these can stay another season without being given more space between them. And that's a problem I'll have to get over in any case – whether or not I stay on.'

There was nothing helpful Anne could say on that brief encounter. Edging away, with her resolve coming to mind, she made what she felt was a trite remark. 'By the way,' he added with a grin, 'those books you lent me are just the sort I needed. I've begun all three because I like to read a chapter of one and then have a think about it before switching on to another. I kind of lose myself in them.'

Anne thought this a rather peculiar way to read books until she realised that her new sense of freedom allowed her to lose herself in what she was now doing solely for herself. A strange phenomenon if one had to lose oneself to become more of a whole personality – to be oneself. Was it, she began to wonder, the one and only way to achieve the wholeness she'd seen in print now and then but failed to see how she could begin to practise it, placed as she was. Of course one had to try and stand outside oneself, to see one's real self, but she'd found it didn't work because there was simply no room to do so with Gerald's bulk and what he stood for, hemming her in on all sides. Perhaps it was that book Spirit of the Valley which was affecting Tom. She remembered when reading it herself last year of feeling disturbed but was unable to see how a member of one sex could entice out, and make good use of, the element of the other sex which the author said was in everyone. At the time such a notion had seemed rather outlandish, but now she had been using what could have been the masculine streak she did not know she possessed, by scheming and standing up to Gerald. It was an interesting subject for further thoughts but the present was no time to indulge in them. She had to go to Dunsford to discuss with Ted Fletcher how to fill in correctly the Ministry's June returns of stocks and crops on the farm. Ted remarked that these had always been a bugbear to her father, who had grappled with them in the past. Now only Ted knew what live and dead stock there was to be recorded.

After two hours, Anne suggested they completed the form next day. This suited Ted, but there was one other matter on which he wanted to have her opinion. They were in the farmhouse kitchen and without another word Ted, a stockily built man in his early fifties, led the way into the back yard. 'I thought it best,' he explained, 'not to bring it up when your mother was around. Not that she won't ever know, but I didn't want to worry her with it.'

'What is it Ted?' Anne asked having had another example of his habit of going all round the houses before coming out with a plain statement.

'Well, it's like this,' he began again. 'You know that double dweller where me and my missus and Ralph live, well, it's all right bar a few little repairs what want doin', but next door, where your father let the old cowman's widder, Mrs Adams live rent free, so long as she were willing to take one o'them student lodgers what come for a year's practice.'

'Yes, I know all that Ted, but what are you trying to tell me?' Anne asked.

'Well, there ee'nt bin a student since your father had his fust attack three year agoo. Not that Mabel Adams minded, 'cos she's well over seventy now, but she's getting hully worried for tew reasons – no, three really. One on account of her age and bein' a bit rheumaticky, and the other that she'd be ashamed if you decided to start having a student each year like your father did.'

'Why ashamed?' Anne prompted.

'On account of the repairs what's needed, the wust one bein' a leaky waterpipe what drips on to the bedroom a student would have to use. That's only recent, and can be cured, but the rooms need redecorating real bad. Time your father were ill, she never said nawthin' and wouldn't have done now 'cos she says she can't complain on account of not paying any rent. But I jest had to tell you Mrs Potts, 'cos nobody else would.'

'Thank you for telling me Ted. I'll go and see her now, and by the way, I want you to drop the Mrs Potts. I'd much rather you just called me Anne, like you used to before I was married, though I believe it got to "Miss Anne" when I left school. You wouldn't want me to call you Mr Fletcher, would you now?'

'No, that I wouldn't M – Anne,' Ted said with a broad grin.

Mabel Adams had the same reluctance to speak in simple terms as did Ted. But having found out the way in which improvements could be made with the least inconvenience to the tenant, she promised to get a decorator and plumber in without delay. The double-dweller – an East Anglian term for semi-detached – flanked the road on one of the smaller farm fields, less than a quarter of a mile from the farmstead, and were the last Dunsford houses on the road to Baldisham.

'There's just one more thing I hain't got off me chest,' said Ted. 'Bin putting it orf like, but it 'as to come. You see, them students – one a year like – used to dew suffn even if they din't dew a lot, and what with one thing and another, there's times when we're real short handed. So would you be of a mind to try and get another one for when Mabel's house is done up – or maybe somebody else to give us a hand. Them local younguns we've got jib at doing overtime. They don't need the extra money, that's why. So another hand wouldn't corst all that much extra, if you see what I mean.'

Looming at the back of Anne's mind was the fact that both Susan and Julian were soon to return for their summer vacation. Not that either were expected to stay all the time at Melthorpe. Julian had, he said, invitations to go and stay with college friends with similar interests to his own in Scotland, Yorkshire and Sussex. Grouse shooting in August appealed to him, but so did Scottish law and land husbandry, but Anne reckoned that if he carried out all his half-made plans, he would be away for most of his vacation before going to Cirencester in September to continue his studies in agriculture. In the present touchy circumstances the less he was at home the better. But to her, Susan's presence would, Anne felt sure, be welcome, not so much as a buffer between her and Gerald on whose side Julian was more than likely to be, but as a confidante when the need arose.

Anne was fully conscious, when she thought about it, that there would still be tensions and pressures difficult to contain, perhaps for a long time to come. Gerald was never one to give in over a prospective deal or a professional dispute, and would certainly be very watchful of any advantage he could gain over her. A holiday for herself was out of the question, and she had no fears that Gerald would suggest going away together as in the past. If he suggested it in their offsprings' hearing, it would be to embarrass or weaken her. He might try just that, and it had worried her until she saw that it could be made to rebound on him. What bothered her most was Susan's idea of going on a camping holiday abroad with a friend. Susan had mentioned this during the last weekend she spent at home, but with so much else on her mind, Anne had given it little thought, especially when Susan said that so far she'd not found a friend at Newnham willing to go with her. Then, on the Friday evening before the Open Sunday, Susan telephoned again.

'Just to check up all's going well with you,' she said gaily, 'and to tell you that I've found a friend to go with abroad, but I'll be home for a week or two before we go.'

'Oh!' Anne said with mixed feelings. 'And who is she – the friend you're going with?'

'Don't be shocked mother, but it's a feller, not a she. Now you needn't begin to worry. He's a well behaved bloke at Trinity, taking Physics. But in any case mother dear, you can trust me to take care of myself. Two females would be more vulnerable, wouldn't they?'

Gerald did not like the idea either, and for a little while they voiced their common concern as if there was no estrangement between them. And then Gerald thumped the dining table firmly with his fist. 'This is just the beginning,' he said in an agonised tone. 'Ever since – well you know what – I've had this fear that one or both of our two would break away because we're no longer a united family. And I can't bear the thought now that Susan has shown what it means to her. She may be going on the loose to show her disgust, but who knows what she'll do next even if she doesn't run into trouble this time. I could well do without additional worries this weekend. Tell me, Anne, are you really so unrepentant as to wittingly let the family fall apart?'

Anne stood up, taking a deep breath. 'If it falls apart Gerald,' she said quite icily, 'it will be as much your fault as mine. But I don't think it will. What you've said has made me remember more clearly what Susan said over the phone. She said, "You can trust me to take care of myself." And that's all I need to know – or have a right to know, now that she's an adult. And as for Julian, he's on your side and how much would it worry you if he took advantage of a girl or two while he's away which caused distress to them – and their parents maybe?'

For the first time ever Anne locked her bedroom door that night. Not that she believed Gerald might resort to violence, but to make sure of not being disturbed in her efforts to simmer down. She knew from his silence that what she'd said had found its mark and this sparked off a new basis for fear. She was strongly tempted to resort again to Mogadons in spite of having recently broken the habit, helped by a little radio and cassette player beside her bed. Several times already she had dropped off with music still playing. Now to ease nagging thoughts she selected Mozart's 23rd Piano Concerto. Settling herself in bed, her range of thought widened in keeping with the events of the day. These, for all the cares they entailed, brought more satisfying feelings. They came as replacements of her former involvements – of supporting Gerald, entertaining his friends, and running his home.

Strangely she was already aware of a deeper attachment with people in and around her new area of activity than she'd ever experienced with Gerald. To find herself suddenly in a position of some authority, to advise, to take positive action for the benefit of others, was to be seen as a duty which brought rewards for herself as well. His world had so often revealed a shallow superficiality which stirred no depth of response in her. But now, having just come through another tussle with him, she felt more certain than ever she was on the right track towards finding her real self. Already she felt stronger than ever before and aware that in winning one tussle it added strength for the next. But she still could not be at all sure that it was the masculine element in her make-up which could have come to her aid. It didn't really make sense when she felt wholly female. Nor could Gerald's less aggressive, dominating attitude be put down to anything other than premeditated ploys to get under her skin, playing on her feminine emotions.

The second movement of the Concerto usually touched her deeply, but now it brought silent tears. They came with a descending peace and gratitude for whatever it was that had given her a strength she did not know she possessed.

Chapter Eight

Tom Berkeley's anxiety over his future as head gardener at Melthorpe was beginning to weigh unbearably heavy. It was accentuated by the knowledge that his marriage was ending. Shirley had been taken on immediately at the new hotel on the A11 highway, and had more than merely hinted she would stay on even if Tom did not. With mounting frustration over his job now that he knew he and Shirley would soon be parting for good, Tom felt a desperate need to know.

During that Open Sunday he forced himself to be pleasant and helpful to those who came to the plant stall. Whenever Gerald spoke to him during the day when on his constant perambulations, his somewhat offhand manner did not change, other than to show up the difference between master and man when visitors were standing by the stall.

On the Monday when Gerald returned from banking the takings, Tom remarked how busy he had been and what few plants had been left unsold. 'I could have sold more of some kinds,' Tom said suggestively, 'and I was wondering if more couldn't be specially grown next year sir.'

'I may decide to do so Berkeley, but I have to tell you that you won't be the grower. I want you to leave on October the first. It means I want the house left vacant by that date, ready for your successor.'

'But sir –' Tom choked, 'I – I thought I was doing a good job for you here. You haven't told me a reason why I have to go. And what about my plants? Can you give me extra time if –.'

'I don't have to give a reason Berkeley, but you've just come out with it yourself. Your precious plants are one reason. While they mean so much to you, you can't give your whole mind to my garden. It proves you're unsuitable to maintain the garden as I wish. I'll be advertising this time for a man who will be quite single-minded – which you're not.'

There was nothing more for Tom to say in his own defence, but for the first time in his life he felt a surge of quite violent emotions. As it was, because Gerald still held the whip hand, he could but plead again for time to remove his plants both from the cottage garden and the kitchen plot. They would still be in full growth and would not move or travel to another site without risk of loss.

Gerald appeared to be quite unmoved as Tom explained. 'Really Berkeley,' he said, 'you should have foreseen such a risk when you decided to bring them with you on to my property. I'll make no promises because it's entirely up to you. I must even remind you that there's no written agreement so far as those plants are concerned and I could legally claim them as mine if I chose to do so. So you'd better bear that in mind.'

Tom wondered how a man for whom he'd done his best could be so hard and implacable. But he was not to know that Gerald still suspected there had been some form of collusion between him and Anne.

Tom realised as he churned over his problems that Anne was the only person to whom he could appeal. Situated as the manor and cottages were on a by-road away from the little village, he had no other contacts. There was not even a pub where he might have gone, and his failure to find anyone willing to let a plot for his plants had put him out on a limb.

Although it was known abroad that Anne was taking control of her father's farm, only hearsay filtered down to Tom. He decided this was the reason why she had not gone as usual to London with the major, but no inkling of any estrangement between them had leaked out.

On the Monday the blow fell for Tom he saw nothing of Anne all day, except when she went out in her car before his encounter with Gerald. But having seen Gerald leave in his Jaguar on Tuesday morning, he began to hope fervently that she would be around.

She, too, drove out soon after Gerald, but was back again at lunchtime. Tom was dead-heading the roses when he saw her walking across the big lawn towards him.

'Hullo Tom,' she said quietly with a smile. 'I had to come as soon as I could to say how sorry I am. It must have hit you hard, and I can but hope you'll find another employer who will appreciate your skill and hard work more than my husband. Did he give you a reason?'

'Not really. Only that he decided my plants were a handicap because they mean a lot to me, making me less up to his standard, sort of thing. But it was no use me arguing with him. He'd made up his mind and that was that.'

'I tried my best, too,' Anne condoned. 'The only admission he made was that he would never have engaged you had he known you were so devoted to your plants – which didn't really register with me. My advice would be to advertise for another post as soon as you can. If you'll draft an advertisement I'll get it typed and sent off, if that'll help. Surely there must be lots of people with big gardens who would be only too glad to take you and a share in your plant collection?'

'There should be,' Tom said, running his fingers through his hair. 'But,' he added, 'wouldn't that make an ad. a bit long and complicated – and expensive. Not that I'd need to stipulate a house to go with the job this time.'

'Why's that?'

'Well,' Tom gave a rueful grin, 'you see Shirley's decided to go her own way. Got a job at a new hotel near Attleborough and wants to stay close to her folks. Suits me, and I don't much mind where I go, so long as I can keep my plants and do something better with them than just heel them in. I'd dearly love to be somewhere where I could do some propagating.'

Anne puckered her forehead. 'But is that very likely?' she mused. 'It seems to me there would be restrictions on increasing them to any extent in even a very large private garden. You might have more trouble with the owner if you made such a request – to produce more than was needed for the garden, I mean.'

'Maybe, but I don't see any other way out. I've thought and thought until my brain seizes up. I've even thought of applying for a job in some hardy plant nursery where I could take them and propagate them. But that's out because no nurseryman would wear that. He'd only take me on if I agreed to sell him all the stock for his own purposes, and I can't bear to part with the only things I possess in this world – what I can call my own.'

'Then what about a National Trust Garden?' Anne suggested. 'Surely one of them, like Blickling or – or Anglesey Abbey would be glad to come to some kind of agreement with you. What you propagated could be distributed to some of the Trust's other gardens. How about that? Would you like me to make some enquiries?'

Tom look intently into her eyes, which till now he had tended to avoid as he had on previous occasions. 'That's a possibility,' he said thoughtfully. 'It's one I hadn't thought of before, and it might be the answer, if it can be fixed up in time – which is very limited by the way the major spoke yesterday. October the first is his deadline date. And he said something else that upset me more than a little. He may not have told you.'

'What was that?'

'Just that he could claim legal ownership of my plants because there's nothing in writing. With all respect, Mrs Potts, I took that very hard.'

Anne moved her head from side to side and clicked her tongue. 'Oh dear! As a matter of fact he did tell me, Tom, and I didn't like it either. But, before we go any further, please drop the Mrs Potts. I'd much rather you call me Anne in future. I can see you're in a tight spot and I want to do anything I can to help. I must go now, and it's your lunchtime too, so let's both have a good think and I'll come and see you again before leaving off time.'

Leaving Tom with glimmers of hope, Anne sped off again after lunch, leaving no room for him guessing where or why. Anne had in fact an appointment with a man from a firm in Attleborough able to undertake the work needed to be done to Mabel Adams' cottage in Dunsford. With old Mabel in attendance, the man wrote down all that needed to be done inside and out with the promise that if his estimate was accepted workmen would be on the job within a few days.

When he'd gone, Anne told Mabel to sit down because there was something she wished to ask her. Anne too sat down and looking into Mabel's plump features wide-eyed in expectation, asked if she would be willing to take a lodger when her house was refurbished.

'Well, Miss Anne,' she mumbled, 'I wouldn't say no to taking a student again like I used to if he could do a few things for hisself 'cos – well, I arnt getting any younger and arnt so nimble as I were.'

'Not a student Mabel, but a man of forty odd who I'm sure you'd find helpful. He's a gardener I know quite well. But whether or not you'll take him, you must promise to say nothing to anyone. I'll get him to come and see you, shall I, if you're agreeable?'

Mabel's face had lit up. 'If he's a man you can speak for, then I'll be glad to have him. After what you're doing for me, I'll do anything for you Miss Anne, that I will. Now, let me make you a cuppa tea and p'raps you'll tell me what I ought to charge him for his keep, allowing for me not paying any rent – unless you think now I should.'

With assurances and a few other details settled other than who the prospective lodger was, Anne went outside. The six-cornered field was in process of losing its crop of early potatoes and the lifting machine was close to the little block of land fronting the road. On the headland where she stood watching a tractor and trailer were being loaded with open-ended bags full of smooth white tubers, whilst behind the machine women were gathering up the crop in baskets to be tipped into more bags.

'A fair good crop,' Ted Fletcher said on reaching the end of the row.

'And a fair good price, we hope,' Anne chuckled. 'By the way, Ted,' she added, 'what's the following crop to be in this field?'

He said he'd decided on coleseed rape, which if sown promptly after the potatoes were cleared would fit in well to be harvested before the main grain harvest next year.

'And should be a blaze of yellow next May,' she agreed. She was on the point of asking for a plot in the piece of land near the road next to Mabel's house to be left unsown, but on quick reflection decided not to, to save Ted asking the reason. To turn under a fraction of it after the rape had begun to grow would be a minute loss, whereas an unsown patch might well raise queries as well as weeds. Ted need not know about Mabel's prospective lodger until or unless the house was refurbished. With that in mind she went back to Mabel with a request that no one but her was to know until Anne gave her permission.

'So it's just a secret between you and me, Miss Anne,' Mabel beamed.

'That's it – just you and me.'

It was close to leaving off time when Anne hastened through the garden looking for Tom. Having found him, she suggested he came back about six that evening. 'I'd like to discuss another idea with you. But it will take up more time than either of us have now, and it needs to be in private.' She toned down to a whisper as Trevor and Michael came back to the potting shed to hang up their tools for the day. 'I'll be where we were this morning just after six,' she added.

Tom was already there snipping off the few overblown roses he had missed. He stood wide-eyed and blinking as she unfolded her plan and what she'd already done towards its fulfilment. She'd had a bubbly feeling all day since the idea had first occurred. The decisions she'd had to make as owner of the farm affecting those dependent on her, had combined to present Tom with the perfect solution to his problem. It still puzzled her why Gerald should have been so hard on him – inhumanly so, as if he bore him a deep-seated grudge. All the more satisfaction then for her to be able to get Tom off the hook. Added to all this sudden involvement in the aspirations and welfare of others was proof it gave of having made the right decision in running the farm herself. In the past, anything she wanted to do for others had to be done through Gerald, one way or another. Her joy of being almost a fairy godmother now allowed no room for snags cropping up, and she even had little fantasies such as learning more about Tom's special plants and ways in which she could help him to set up as a specialist nurseryman.

Scarcely noticing the perplexed expression which now and then flitted across his wide-eyed amazement as she spoke, she finally stopped and said, 'Well, Tom, what do you think? Does it appeal to you?'

'It appeals so much,' he replied huskily, 'that I can't quite take it in. It's as if all I ever wanted nearly all my life is being offered to me on a plate, like. Seems to be too good to be true, when I think of what a failure I've been up to now.'

'I think you deserve a break,' Anne soothed.

'But you – you know hardly anything about my past. What bothers me all of a sudden is because you seem to trust me, I've come over afraid I might let you down –.' He tailed off with a worried expression as if this was not his only fear.

'I've no fear on that score, Tom,' she said. 'It's enough to know how hard you've worked here to rule that out, so long as you don't mind working on farm jobs until you get your nursery going to keep you full time.'

Almost chokingly Tom said, 'But I reckon I failed when I set up on my own because I don't have much of a business head. That's what Shirley said too, and if I thought I was sort of sponging – taking advantage of you, like – well I couldn't bear that. But that isn't all, 'cos another thing has just struck me. I didn't think of it while what you said was making me so surprised and excited.'

'What is it?' asked Anne softly, becoming aware of her deflating spirits. She had expected Tom would hold out both hands to grasp the opportunity she had given him, believing it was all so simple, so timely for him and so gratifying to herself by way of a bonus. But now his lack of confidence in himself and his unsuspected scruples were putting a damper on things, making her wonder what else was coming to mar the unique occasion it was for her.

'I hardly like to –' he began awkwardly, 'I mean, I don't know how to put it. But your husband – you must have thought, surely, what his reactions might be? He doesn't like me, and it's worried me because I've done my best. Can't you see what I mean, Anne? I couldn't bear it if he. . . . Do I need to say any more?'

'Are you trying to say it might upset him and make life more difficult for me? Or are you worried about being in the middle of a family row? Is that it?'

'That's about the size of it,' Tom replied. 'It would sort of knock the stuffing out of me from the start, to know that what you were doing for me back-fired on you.'

Anne's head drooped a little. 'Let's go to that seat over there,' she said pensively.

'You mustn't give in, Tom,' Anne said impulsively, patting his hand resting on the seat beside her. 'And now I'm going to be very blunt. If you take up my offer, you'll be doing something for me. I need something like this, if only to be a person in my own right, if you like. It'll be like putting a seal on a declaration of independence, and I'm prepared to face up to whatever may come of it. If it causes a rift, or whatever, it won't be my fault – or wish.'

Anne had been gently rubbing her knees to and fro looking downwards as she spoke. Having had her say, she looked across to Tom's face in time to see tears beginning to drip from his eyes as he hastily drew out his handkerchief to wipe them. She noticed the spasms as he was trying hard to hold down as his head turned away in shame. 'Sorry,' he muttered chokily. 'Couldn't help it. Never thought anybody would do such a thing for me, like you're doing.'

'Oh Tom!' Anne whispered, touching his hand again. 'Don't forget that you'll be doing a lot for me too.'

After a brief silence she stood up, as did Tom. He braced his lean shoulders and smiled as she led the way into the kitchen garden.

'It's very strange,' Anne said quite brightly as they stood near the double doors of the back garden entrance to the lane, with

Tom holding his bicycle, 'your wife and my husband have somehow forced us to come up with a plot and to keep it secret. It's not to harm them, but hopefully to become our true selves. Whether we succeed or not is entirely up to us, isn't it? Goodnight Tom. Sleep well.'

Chapter Nine

Following the very successful Open Sunday in June, Gerald decided to hold a Thursday Garden Fête in late July in aid of more local good causes, including repairs to the church roof. This meant closer attention to watering the garden as the drought persisted, and the investment in more sprinklers for irrigation. Tom was warned not to water his plot without special permission. That this was flouted without him knowing was thanks to Anne, who aided and abetted him in watering after dark. By the midday following the surface soil had dried again, and Gerald never suspected.

The Garden Fête was a great success. It yielded over four hundred pounds for charity, in addition to a hundred which Gerald privily retained so as to make a cash payment for some additional frames in which to grow more bedding plants for sale next year. There had to be a limit, he decided, to what could safely be charged to the farm. Farm crops were suffering on light land fields. Sugar beet drooped their leaves, barley ears were thin and pastures became brown. It would be a poor harvest, which meant that less of the garden expenses could be charged to the farm.

Anne herself found that much closer involvement in what soil, sun and moisture produced was making her, too, feel the effects of the drought. Her own crops at Dunsford were suffering just as much as everyone else's in the area, and all longed for rain to revive both crops and spirits. To see the greenery and colour as a result of ample irrigation over the manor garden brought her anything but amelioration when visiting her farm.

The little river Dun was still flowing, and though much reduced, there was enough for her to suggest to Ted Fletcher that an irrigation pump would be worth installing. Ted then explained that her father had applied for the necessary permission five years before, but it had been refused on the grounds that it would adversely affect other farmers in the lower reaches. What was needed, he added, was a deep borehole to tap the water bearing chalk strata far below, though this too required a licence.

A severe thunderstorm came late in July and though half an inch of rain fell, it was such a downpour that much of it ran off, failing to penetrate the bone dry top layer of soil. But if hopes rose that this heralded the end of the dry spell, more sunny days prevailed to renew anxieties. If there was abundant water down below in the chalk, Anne reasoned, then it would be worth the cost to have it brought up for irrigation against future droughts even if procedures took too long to bring relief for this one. She had a few thousand in her secret deposit account at the bank, saved over the years out of Gerald's allowance, which would go a long way towards an artesian borehole and pump.

On second thoughts, there might well be another use for some of her money. Tom had expressed fears that the two hundred or so kinds of plants he was keeping alive would need augmenting if he were to aim for a mail order type of nursery.

Anne agreed that local demand would not be worth considering. Having made this mistake in Surrey, he'd got to build up a stock in wide variety of the less common kinds, and then advertise from a catalogue. Anne guessed that he hadn't the money to invest in more stock, and because this was a worry to him, she decided to offer some as an investment. But not yet. He was feeling beholden to her quite enough already, and such an offer might be more than he could take, however much the thought of a new and interesting involvement appealed to her.

A more immediate concern came from Mabel Adams asking her every week or two when her lodger would be coming, now that improvements to her house were completed. Gerald had somehow come to know about these and even commended Anne in a half sarcastic way that it was one of the facets of good husbandry to have workers tied cottages fit to live in.

'Did you know,' he queried, 'that rent restrictions on tied agricultural cottages applied only when occupied by a worker on the farm? A widow of a former worker doesn't qualify, so why don't you turn her out and let it to your foreman's son, who I hear is your best tractor driver and wants to get married.'

It was the first time for several weeks that Gerald had made any reference to Anne's new interest. She, in turn, had responded as best she could to what seemed to be a truce, albeit an uneasy one liable to be fractured again very soon. It made sense to avoid provocation in the hope that the next stage, in which Tom would figure, would be less traumatic.

There were also Julian, and even more, Susan to consider. They were at home on and off during the long vacation and it was up to her as their mother to try her utmost to keep the family intact. She also had to keep future plans involving Tom a secret. Even though Susan might be trusted to side with her, she dare not take any risks. So it was that she did not rise to Gerald's curious reference to Mabel's tenancy. Though his interference made her bridle, she glibly forced a smile and told him that she'd talked it over with Ted, whose advice was to take Mabel's offer to have a student type of helper again and that his son and prospective wife were planning to find a home of their own. It was not too much of an untruth, because Gerald had promptly dropped the subject and went on to enquire how her mother was getting on with the parson Revd Hemming and his bride.

'Very well indeed,' Anne said briskly. 'Mother's always had a soft spot for romances and theirs appeals to her all the more because they've had to wait so long, and because he's a clergyman. She likes him as a person even if he's a bit unorthodox, and she told me the longer it takes to build a new vicarage for them, the better she'll be pleased. She finds Claire helpful as well as good company.'

'I'm glad it's all working out so well,' Gerald said, in such a way that Anne was tempted to make some caring enquiry about his own domestic arrangements at the London flat. She had pieced together odd snippets he'd dropped over past weeks that he was making the best of what was for him a bad job. She guessed he was having to employ a part-time woman each day, in spite of having his lunch and dinner out. It was no longer her concern, was the impression he gave her, and what she herself believed, nor was it for her to question why his London visits had of late become more erratic in timing and duration. This was a factor which put her more on her guard than had he stuck to the old routine. It forced her to be somewhat clandestine in her contacts with Tom when future plans for him had to be discussed.

Tom himself was on edge. Now and again his rather gaunt features and deep-set eyes betrayed excitement at his prospects, so much changed for the better, but sometimes there were signs of his frustrations. These Anne could understand enough to offer sympathy and encouragement, but because he told her so little of the situation between himself and Shirley, she wondered if complications had arisen which would affect her plans for him. It was not, she decided, for her to interfere between husband and wife, and if they were having second thoughts about parting for good, then she must abide by any decision they made, even if it upset her half secret plans. It made her feel as if she was on a see-saw, until one morning in early September.

From a distance she caught sight of him working like a madman with a fork. He was keeping his head down and bent almost double. His two helpers were disappearing into the potting shed carrying bags of what she guessed were potatoes. Coming closer she called, 'Why the hurry Tom?' He quickly stood up and gave her the broadest of grins, leaning forward on his fork.

'She's gone!' he said in a loud excited whisper. 'She's gone and won't be coming back!' Calming down he explained that on returning home after work the day before he found some of the furniture had vanished along with the television, some cutlery and crockery, with a note put by the bed stating that she was leaving him for good.

'Obviously you're glad,' Anne smiled slightly, to sober him down.

'I can't tell you just how glad I am. These past three weeks have been nearly enough for me to do the leaving. But now I know I'm free, and I had to let rip after moping about last evening trying to tidy up and take stock of myself, wishing I could come and tell you.'

'Trevor and Michael are on the way back,' she reminded him. 'Let's have another talk this evening. I'll be alone. Gerald left early this morning and both Susan and Julian are away. We've got to plan the next move very carefully.' Then she added, 'Same place at six o'clock – seat near the sundial?'

Tom was waiting looking down on to the sundial with the usual inscription when Anne came towards him.

> The kiss of the sun for pardon,
> The song of the birds for mirth,
> You're nearer God's heart in a garden
> Than anywhere else on earth.

'Does the inscription fit?' Anne asked.

'It never stirred me,' he admitted, 'though I did try to see it that way. It might have done so in some gardens, but not this one, even if I feel more peaceful in my mind than for a long time. Sometimes I doubt if there is a God at all.'

'So do I Tom, but I also think it depends on whether or not you want to believe there is.'

'I used to believe what they taught me about God. I used to go to church and say my prayers every night, but none were ever answered so I gave up. I'm a humanist if anything.'

'And I'm just an agnostic, but let's get down to business shall we?' Anne said firmly.

Half an hour later Tom was sitting beside her on the way to Dunsford, having decided the time had come to make arrangements with Mabel Adams. To become her lodger would leave the gardener's house empty. This, Anne thought, should suit Gerald rather than cause an upset, because he could then offer vacant possession to whom he selected as the replacement for Tom. His stock of plants left for a little longer in two places should be no inconvenience to anyone and he could begin moving them over to Dunsford by degrees as weather permitted. As if to add a blessing to these plans, it began to rain gently as they left Melthorpe for the two mile journey. Leaving the Volvo on the roadside, they hurried down the short path to shelter under the little front door porch.

'Why! If it isn't Miss Anne,' Mabel Adams exclaimed. 'And is the gentleman the one –.'

'It is Mabel. May we come in?'

Having chattered, all three went up to see the room Tom was to have and the tiny bathroom Anne's father had installed ten years before which halved the size of the small third bedroom. Another chat downstairs over a cup of Nescafé which Mabel insisted on making, and it was past eight o'clock when they were on their way back to Melthorpe. It was still raining, but not as heavily as either of them wished.

As they entered the drive, heading for the double garage at the rear of the house, they could see Gerald's Jaguar occupying its usual half. Casting a swift glance at the back door, Anne saw it open to reveal him standing, staring, just as Tom stepped out into the glare of the outside light which Gerald had switched on.

'Off you go! I can handle it,' whispered Anne.

Having closed the garage door to give her more time to think, she found Gerald in the lounge pouring himself a drink. He gave her a look of supercilious amusement and quite calmly explained that he'd decided to return in order to fit in two interviews with prospective head gardeners arranged next day. After a sip, he went to the mantlepiece, selected a cigar taking longer than usual to prepare and light it, and looked across now and then with the same sardonic smile before he spoke. After the first puff he then said he'd had a meal at a Little Chef on the way home, so she had only her own to see to. 'Unless, of course, you've been out for a meal with Berkeley?' he added with unmistakeable sarcasm.

Anne shot him what she thought was a warning glance.

Gerald took up his glass and followed her along the passage to the kitchen. 'You don't wish to tell me where you've been with Berkeley? I suppose,' he challenged.

'I see no reason why I should,' she countered.

'I think you'd better do so,' he persisted, 'before I jump to conclusions. Or would you rather I guessed?'

Anne's gorge rose swiftly. 'You can think what the hell you like Gerald.' Then checking herself with the thought that he was being deliberately provocative she added, 'If you must know – no – I'm hanged if I'll tell you! I don't pry into your affairs and you've no right to pry into mine. I've nothing disloyal to confess and if you'll leave me alone, you'll soon learn the reason. I'm just not ready to tell you yet, so why not let it drop?'

Gerald snorted with, 'If you're up to mischief affecting me, and the family, you'll pay dearly for it, believe you me. And if I can't make you talk now, I've a few weapons still up my sleeve. You've insulted me and I don't like it.' At the door of his study Gerald turned and called back to Anne as she made for the handsome staircase to go to her room, holding her toasted cheese sandwich. 'If you decide to come clean,' he said coldly, 'I have my first interview at ten thirty tomorrow. My advice to you is to think carefully before morning just where your stupid intrigue is leading. You've confirmed now the suspicions I've had of your liaison with Berkeley. And if you're intending to make the most of the time he's got left here, then I can – well, I still hold the whip hand, don't I?'

It was too early for bed and sleep would be elusive anyway. Neither reading nor listening to music would ease Anne's whirling thoughts nor dispel the anger which gnawed at her, undermining her confidence. She had been tripped up just when things were going well. Her impulsive reaction of stubbornly refusing to divulge the reason for Tom being with her had brought an additional burden to carry. By not telling Gerald what was afoot, she now began to realise that she had made it harder to do so when the time came. His threats might lack substance, but they showed up a jealousy she'd not expected simply because she knew there was no cause for him to be jealous.

Anne found herself beginning to hate Gerald. Looking back she began to doubt whether she had ever loved him, but had put him on a pedestal when he first made advances to her, and somehow had seen him as an ideal husband when he asked her to marry him. The long years of trying to be his ideal wife had blinkered her estimation of him as a person shorn of his pretensions. It was not until she began to feel the emptiness and lack of purpose in her own life and personality that she began to grow up and see the man behind his facade of benevolent geniality combined with gentlemanly respectability. He had gained his ends through this, but beneath was the schemer. His masculine aggression and dominance were so controlled as to acquire power and wealth, without her and others being aware of it as they came under his spell. Now that she had at last rumbled him, she wanted to hit back. And she'd found that in asserting her independence she had gained more success by adopting his own scheming methods than by pleading her cause with him.

In advising her to come clean over her involvement with Tom, she now saw that this was consistent with Gerald's earlier attempts to undermine her resolve. To come out now with her plans for Tom would strengthen his position but weaken hers.

When Anne came down having overslept when sleep finally came, she found that Gerald had had his breakfast and his coffee cup had gone. As she sat down to toast and marmalade he came through holding his empty cup. 'I'll have a second one if there's enough in the pot,' he said quite calmly, his features betraying nothing. 'Ah! Only half a cup left, but never mind.' Still standing he looked at her as he sipped. 'Well, Anne. Now that you've had, I hope, a good night's sleep, have you anything to tell me? It's my concern for our good name and to avoid family disunity which affects me so deeply.' His tone, quiet and almost conciliatory was disarming.

'I really don't think I need add anything to what I said last night. Except perhaps that I feel rather sorry for Tom and am doing what I can to make his leaving easier. It's all above board as I'm sure you will agree, when the time comes to tell you.'

'Why can't you tell me now?'

'I've told you why I prefer not to. It's entirely my affair anyway, Gerald. And I've told you before I think you've been pretty hard on him.'

'Not at all,' he replied blandly, 'I consider he came here under rather false pretences, assuring me that he would play his full part in keeping up my traditional way of gardening. But what does he do but ask me for land for growing his choice of plants – and you've aided and abetted him.' He paused, and as his expression changed, narrowing his eyes and tightening his thick lips, he hastily tipped off the rest of his coffee and left her with, 'Have it your own way then,' and stalked out.

All day, much of which she spent at Dunsford, the thought assailed Anne that Gerald, with so many irons in the fire, should have become almost paranoid about such a relatively trivial matter. And it was brushing off on to her, forcing her in countering it to make it a vital issue. She walked down the lane and found Tom in the little cottage garden trimming the stems from plants which had finished flowering.

'I'm glad you've come,' he greeted her anxiously. 'I gather you had to spill the beans.'

'I certainly did not,' she protested in alarm. 'Why? – Has he wormed it out of you instead?'

Tom's face took on a sadly lugubrious expression. 'He spoke just as if you had told him,' he muttered. 'Began by saying he didn't blame me for accepting your help with my plants. If you didn't tell him where they were going, he must have guessed. Oh hell! Have I made it difficult for you? The last thing I want to do is to let you down, or come between you and your husband.'

'Let's go indoors Tom,' she advised. 'We're a bit conspicuous out here. He said he was going back to London, but let's see if we can make good the damage – if any. After all, it had to come out pretty soon. Did he say anything else?'

'Yes, and it's an added worry on top of the rest. I know I should have guessed you'd not told him the plan, but what hit me below the belt was him saying my plants must not be moved elsewhere without his permission. When I asked why, he said he had his own reasons, and besides, the plants were now his because they were on his property. Anne, what's he up to? Why should he have such a grudge against me?'

'I don't know. I just don't know,' she said. 'But it seems he's got a grudge against us both, and if it's bluff, then we must find a way of calling it.'

It was the first time Anne had been inside the cottage since Tom and Shirley came to live there. Its bareness as a result of Shirley taking more than half the furniture emphasised the smallness of its rooms. Her sympathy for Tom increased as she noticed that he'd attempted to make it more habitable for himself and there was no unwashed clutter at the sink. 'What have you had for a meal?' she asked.

'Sardines,' he grinned. 'But I'll have to do some shopping pretty soon, just to last me till I can go to Mrs Adams.'

'The sooner you do that the better,' Anne said decisively.

Chapter Ten

On his journey back to London that evening, Gerald was glad he'd not fallen to the temptation to double back in hopes of catching Anne and Tom together. What he'd said to each of them was surely enough to make them realise that it did not pay to take risks with him. If Tom had any concern for his own welfare and if Anne had any sense of loyalty and duty left, his warnings should have sunk in to good effect. None the less, his anxieties had remained too acute to spend the night at Melthorpe. Time and again there came back to nag him the thought of a sexual attraction between the two of them, for all Anne's assurance. She had never shown the kind of response in bed towards him he would have wished. She had always been so passive towards his advances.

There was no accounting for women's ways but he had to take account of the wide gap in age. Yet it wasn't only sexual relations. There were other intimacies such as holding hands and kissing. Her hands had become limp in his long ago, and if he'd got accustomed to the way she avoided her lips on his by offering her cheek, such things all added up, along with her recent waywardness. It forced him to see her as she really was, which was very different to the person she pretended to be before he married her, and until well after the children came along. He'd seen her nurturing of them as they grew up as too casual, leaving them too often to make their own way and choices. It was a wonder that they'd turned out as well as they had, but his own influence had undoubtedly been attributable to this, although Susan was too much of a modern girl.

There was so much to be said, Gerald believed, for the older values and traditions and there was ample evidence to be seen of a decadence coming as a result of modern laxity. He firmly believed that England's greatness which lasted till about 1950, was due to the moral fibre of the nation till then. Class distinctions were necessary for stability and prosperity. Higher standards of living for the working class had brought inflation and indolence on their part. The Empire had been frittered away, along with the once formidable British navy; the crime rate had rocketed and sexual permissiveness had become established, aided by the Pill, which he now suspected had prevented him from fathering a second son. He also believed that women's emancipation had gone much too far. They were not equipped by their very nature to be other than subservient to men. Nor should they be allowed to enter men's traditional domain. There were of course a few exceptions, and he had to admit that the leader of the Party he supported was showing, by some genetic freak, that she had more male than female in her make-up.

Gerald was tired when he let himself into his flat and a stiff whisky dulled his uneasy mind. Within minutes of his alarm clock ringing next morning, the telephone bell also rang.

'Charlotte Norton here – you remember?'

'Of course I do,' Gerald answered briskly. 'Where are you and how are you? I've been hoping to hear from you again.'

Charlotte explained that now that her legacy of the saleable contents of Marlington Hall had been removed to Critchleys' London storage in readiness for the auction, she was coming up to London with John who was flying back to New Zealand that afternoon. Now that offers were trickling in both for parts or the whole of the estate, John was satisfied that Gerald's firm could see the sale through without him hanging about any longer. 'Can we meet?' she added. 'I'd like to take you up on your offer to help me find somewhere to live. It's become rather urgent because the friend I was going to stay with while I looked around has had to go into hospital unexpectedly.'

'Um! Well, yes,' Gerald said, 'I'm pretty busy this morning, but I could be available this afternoon.'

It came as a welcome relief to have something to look forward to and he began to make some plans. By the time they were having tea at the Royal Court Hotel in Sloane Square where Charlotte intended to book in for the night, his plan was completed.

'I have a flat in mind that might suit you,' he said with a subdued smile. 'And I could take you to it as a first step. Afterwards would it appeal to you to be my guest for dinner at a very good restaurant I know – or come back here where the menu is probably as good?'

Charlotte chose his first suggestion and having booked a room was being shown round Gerald's own flat fifteen minutes later. He explained his situation at some length before telling her that because he was now its sole occupant, for about three nights a week, it had become quite ridiculous to stay on. It would be cheaper and more congenial in a hotel. And although he was almost decided on this point, he was still hesitating.

Charlotte showed sympathy but was anxious to know what the rent would be, a question she had to repeat for lack of a direct answer the first time.

'It may appear somewhat precipitous,' he demurred, 'but since you've been looking round and showing interest, it has occurred to me to make a rather outlandish proposition. I hope you'll not be offended.'

'Well, well, let's hear it!' Charlotte exclaimed.

'I'd be happy to forgo any rent if you would accept me as an occasional lodger – no lunches required and no hard and fast obligations for dinner either. Frankly Charlotte – if I may use your first name — it would be the ideal solution for me, but I won't press you. Do feel perfectly free to decide.'

Charlotte's dark eyes narrowed, giving him a searching look. 'And what,' she asked with the vestige of a smile, 'would the rent be as a vacant, furnished flat? On my own, I mean.'

It was a question Gerald did not expect.

'Well –' he hesitated, 'as I told you I own the whole house. The tenants on the ground floor and the one above have their own furniture and they pay eighty and sixty respectively – a week, that is. This one would be cheap at a hundred, furnished as it is, don't you think? The rates, which I pay, are pretty stiff.'

Charlotte paced around tapping her fingertips together and wearing a far away expression. 'Let's go and eat,' she said finally. 'But don't rush me for an answer. I may be able to give it before I go back to the hotel.'

Her conversation during the meal was as if she had no decision to make. She spoke about Marlington, how sad she was to leave it and how she was depending on good results from the sale of her only assets from her legacy at Critchleys' auction next week. She smoked four cigarettes before the leisurely meal was finally ended. And as he held out her lightweight mac to cover her thin blue dress, she tapped his hand saying, 'I'll take your offer Gerald,' in a surprisingly matter of fact tone, 'but with a month's mutual trial of course.'

He had to check himself from thanking her. Her decision had given him a peculiar sense of uplift, making him aware of how much he needed such a fillip just now. It was not quite a case of drawing a bow as a venture finding its mark. Ever since Anne's refusal to spend the London stays with him any more, he had come to see such a recourse as nothing but his due, with no slur on him should it result in cohabitation with a woman. But it would much more likely to have been one below his own social standing, and now thanks to the good impression he must have made when they first met weeks ago, the thought of her aristocratic background was something to be savoured. The utmost prudence, however, was needful. It would have been very imprudent if he'd given in to the fleeting temptation to suggest Charlotte should cancel her hotel booking and stay the night, since her luggage had been transferred to his car so that she could garage hers. She had forgotten this fact when she booked a room, and in his eagerness he had not reminded her. Yes, it would be imprudent, he reminded himself again, but it came as a relief when she asked if she could take up residence next morning and take only her overnight case to the hotel.

'My first business appointment tomorrow is ten thirty,' he told her, 'May I pick you up at nine-thirty? By then I'll have the rest of your luggage taken up. I have a spare key and I expect you'll need to do some shopping later, and I don't have to go back to Melthorpe until Friday. And what about cash for victuals? Stocks are pretty low and I must pay my whack. Would fifty be enough I wonder?'

With all arranged amicably, they settled down that next evening with a look of contentment on both their faces. 'That was a most excellent dinner you cooked,' Gerald remarked over his glass of Cognac. With all the tact he could muster he encouraged her to tell him of her past. She had been married to Major Norton for nine years but all too frequent postings to Germany, Cyprus and Northern Ireland had made life increasingly difficult for her, and raising a family with no permanent home base was not on, so far as she was concerned. The rift began, she said, because there was not, nor could be, the kind of family life she craved, and her husband having become a brigadier at thirty-eight as well as a baronet on the death of his impoverished father, was too dedicated to the army, and she decided to divorce him. 'And since it came through,' she went on, 'I've spent almost all my time with John who is virtually my only relative – in England, that is. We women do seem to get snared one way and another, don't we?'

'Some men would say it was the other way round,' he joked, but then switched by saying that he fully understood and appreciated how she felt.

Charlotte made no further comment, taking time to tap and then light another cigarette, inhaling deeply before she spoke again. 'I envy your wife Gerald. From what I gather she was very young when she had her babies. I'm thirty-five now and prospects of a family aren't good.' Her wistful expression changed as she continued after another pause. 'I'll just have to get weaving, won't I? You probably guessed why I wanted to live in London, though hopefully not for good. And you did say I'd be free to entertain my own friends, didn't you?'

'Of course,' Gerald answered. But her remarks had chilled the hopes he'd been nursing.

After some thought, Gerald decided to drop a hint. 'I can't help being touched,' he said gently, 'by what you said about family life. You see, that's always been my ideal too and although I have a son and daughter, my wife seems intent on undermining what means so much to me.'

'How do you mean – undermining?'

'Perhaps that's not quite the right word,' he continued. 'Anne was never strongly – well – maternal, and now that Julian and Susan are more or less making their own way in life, she appears to be intent on doing likewise. I'll admit she was pretty good as housekeeper and hostess, but it lacked something. Dedication, I think. You'll know what I mean. I fancy the legacy of her father's little farm was just the excuse she's been waiting for and she's using it to opt out of coming here three days a week.'

'Which let me in,' Charlotte smiled enigmatically.

Gerald, having begun, decided to continue regardless. 'I'm doing my utmost to keep the family intact. But it's not easy when one vital member seems to be out of step – even to having clandestine meetings with my head gardener, who's under notice to leave at the end of the month.' Gerald stopped abruptly, aware that he'd said quite enough to put her in the picture.

Changing the subject completely, he suggested that they checked Critchleys' auction catalogue in which Charlotte's legacies from Marlington Hall were included. Due to some misunderstanding with the V. & A. Museum, it was a shorter list than she'd hoped and anticipated. Her uncle had made a written promise to leave several items to the Museum, but the letter had not been produced until the sale was announced. And Charlotte had put some pieces into store in hopes of a home of her own. Her eyes lit up when Gerald offered to attend the auction with her. Then she said it was time for bed, and giving his knuckles a friendly squeeze, and a 'See you in the morning', she walked across to what had been Anne's bedroom which, like his own, had its own bathroom and toilet.

Gerald was wakeful with many and often conflicting thoughts. Remembering that both Julian and Susan would be at home for their last few days of vacation, he fell asleep with his mind made up that parental duty as well as prudence must take first place.

Arriving home in the early evening, it set the tone for a happy family weekend to find Anne, as well as Julian and Susan, enjoying themselves in the swimming pool. And throughout the long weekend he and Anne appeared to be equally conscious of the need to promote family unity. Her efforts made him wonder if she'd finally seen the error of her ways. Actions spoke louder than words, and her attitude towards him was as if there had been no quarrel at all to which he could not help respond, with the same easy acceptance shown by Julian and Susan. The name Berkeley was never mentioned, not did Anne spend any time at the farm on her own. When both Julian and Susan said they'd like to see it and their grandmother, Anne even asked Gerald to join them, but he politely declined on the grounds that preparations had to be made for the last Open Sunday in a week's time.

It came as a surprise at breakfast next morning however to hear his suggestion that they should go to church as a family. 'We've none of us been since the new parson came and it's an opportunity to give him some encouragement.'

'I bet he needs it,' Susan said, 'Grandma says he's a nice enough man but too much of a modern for her liking, as a parson, that is. Well, I'm willing to go if mother and Julian are.'

Neither of them had any wish to go but did not have the heart to refuse such a demonstration of family unity. Only a score of other worshippers were present as they sat in some isolation in the front pew which went as a manorial right. Yet Gerald obviously enjoyed having the loudest voice of anyone as they sang the hymns. Susan said afterwards that she found Peter Hemming's ten minute sermon on human links with God and nature quite stimulating, whilst Julian wondered how such a man could stick such a downgrade job. Anne made no comment. The Second Lesson had included the Parable of the Talents and she preferred to keep its message to herself.

Gerald returned to London on the Tuesday, just after Julian had left to begin his year at Cirencester. Susan was due to leave next day, and Anne felt that the bond between her and Susan had become stronger than it had ever been. At the back of her mind for almost a week had been the warning Gerald had given to Tom about the ownership of his plants. It loomed now as a threat, not only to Tom but to herself. The thought of sponsorship had appealed first to help a man down on his luck, and secondly to a nursery becoming an additional source of interest to her. Tom's past failures were in support of a growing belief that she, rather than he, possessed the key to success on the commercial side. Her emerging drive and business acumen, which had come already with her running the farm, had surprised her as well as her mother and Ted Fletcher. Tom would be the expert in cultivation and production, with her a willing enthusiastic learner, whilst she would also be the business head when it came to having enough to sell. This would take time – a year or more, Tom had said. It would also need capital outlay for buying in more variety for stock. Tom's two hundred kinds would be only a part of what would be required to produce an attractive catalogue and bring in orders. Tom had very little by way of capital, but she had enough to get the project going and was prepared to use it to make her a full, active partner.

Anne had discussed these matters with Tom when she took him to see the site. It took a little time to reassure him, but when she knew his hesitation was on her behalf, she made it plain that what she was offering to do was in line with her own hopes and ambitions as well and his reservations vanished. She added that she'd be willing to have a proper partnership agreement drawn up for mutual protection. At this, Tom, with some emotion showing, declared that his trust in her was enough for him. This left its mark on her emotions and she'd reflected often that such a trust had never before been her lot. Even her parents had never fully trusted her judgement. Nor had Gerald, because what she did for him always sprang from his wishes or initiative, and his compliments on her efficiency had, she realised, been a means of keeping her up to his standards. And once she also realised fully that Tom's unspoken need of her was becoming more and more matched by her need of what he could supply to develop her own talents and personality, then the way forward became clear and enticing.

The indications were that Gerald had no intention of holding his usual autumn and winter shooting parties. She had a suspicion that by not inviting people to come in summer over the past few weeks was in hopes of putting her to shame. To some extent maybe this was because his Open Sundays for garden visitors was giving him more satisfaction, judging by the way his enthusiasm for them had increased.

Then came the thought, out of the blue, that the reason why he had laid claims to owning Tom's plants could be some notion he'd come up with, to include them in what would be offered for sale to the visitors. And much as she tried to dismiss the thought that he'd play such a dirty trick on Tom, it nagged her persistently. Especially when looking round she found very little by way of plants, indoor or out, which were surplus and saleable. The soft fruit had finished and apples were not yet ready to pick.

Anne sought out Tom saying they must talk.

'Has something happened?' Tom asked anxiously.

'No, but it might if we don't act quickly. Tell me, Tom, are those plants of yours – any of them I mean – fit for sale as they are?'

Responding to the look in her eyes, he refrained from first asking why, before answering her question. 'Some are, where they're not flowering. But why? You're not suggesting we need or want to sell them are you?'

'Not us – but someone else might think they would sell on the stall next Sunday. Had that occurred to you? Maybe that's the reason why Gerald said they were legally his.'

Tom's eyes narrowed. 'Good God!' he muttered. 'I never thought of that. I can't really believe he'd stoop to such a thing. I thought he said it just to sort of put some sort of screws on me. But if that's what you think —.'

'It's a possibility we can't ignore Tom,' Anne broke in. 'But it'll put the cat amongst the pigeons if we do the only thing to avoid it.'

'You mean – move them to your farm? But when?'

Anne had already decided because she saw no other way. 'Do you still have the boxes they came in?'

'Yes,' Tom nodded. 'Stacked up against the outhouse wall.'

'Then let's get them packed, just as soon as we can alter your working hours, even if we have to work after dark. And I'll take a car load down each night.'

Soon after Trevor and Michael had left off work for the day, Anne took a thermos flask of tea and some sandwiches to Tom who had just returned from his cottage with a barrow load of empty trays and boxes. As he ate he told her how to lift each kind gently with a fork, leaving a little earth on their roots and then pack them upright in trays with newspaper between to keep each kind separate. Some had grown larger in spite of the poor conditions, and a few such as cimicifuga and aconitum were in flower, needing extra care. Two hours later as it was growing dark, the plot was empty of plants. And there were more full boxes than the Volvo would hold.

'Land Rover,' Anne said, rubbing her aching back. 'Open the double gates when you hear me coming, and make sure it's me. Thank goodness the lane isn't much used.'

It was quite dark when they backed into the gateway not far from Mabel Adams' cottage. They were unloading the boxes, setting them down behind the low thorn hedge, when Ted Fletcher found them. 'What's afoot?' he asked, then chuckled when Anne told him. 'All right, I'll help you. Sudden emergency, eh? What's the name of that white flower?'

'Can't stop to tell you now, Ted,' Anne said breathlessly. 'We're going back for more. I did tell you last week they were coming soon, didn't I? We just decided not to wait till early October.'

'Better for the plants now,' Tom fibbed light-heartedly now that positive action was in progress.

Back they went to Melthorpe, but having decided it would be too dark to being lifting the plants from Tom's cottage garden, they decided to call it a day. He said he'd be on the job at first light but would be at the Manor garden as usual at eight o'clock.

'In for a penny –' Anne smiled. 'I'll set my alarm two hours forward and come and join you. I'm finding it quite exciting. We can but hope we don't get caught in the act!'

'In any case you'll get as much if not more blame when your husband finds out. That still worries me.'

'Don't let it Tom,' Anne consoled. 'I think I can handle it when it comes – hopefully not until your garden is empty. It's a risk we've got to take and I can't see he can get at you with only two more full weeks to go before you're out of his reach. Stick it out whatever he says or tries to do and you'll come out on top. He's not really vindictive, he just doesn't like to be thwarted and has some rather fixed ideas.'

Chapter Eleven

Had they known that Gerald had a private reason for not returning until the end of the week, it would have been a less hurried and hazardous task for them,. The last load was delivered to Dunsford on Thursday evening. After giving them a good watering Tom said that they would take no harm until he could lay them in the now damp soil over the weekend.

'What if you're expected to take charge of the plant stall?' Anne asked, wondering what his reply would be in the circumstances after the hints she'd given that he should be less timid.

'I won't be available, will I?' he grinned. 'And I doubt if I'll be asked to do any more overtime with only two weeks to go.'

'Good for you! But what will you say if he threatens you for taking the plants away without his permission?'

'Nothing. He's not likely to take me to court, is he? But it's what you'll have to face for aiding and abetting that bothers me. Would you agree to me saying I took time off – the paid holiday time due to me? That might put you in the clear.'

Gerald arrived at dusk on Friday evening. In a jerky voice he said he'd not had time to stop for a meal on the way and would be glad if she would make him an omelette or something.

'Of course,' Anne said.

Gerald then said it was going to be a rush tomorrow to get ready for Sunday opening, but although he hadn't specifically told Tom that his help would be needed on the Saturday, no doubt he would volunteer.

Anne answered as casually as she could that she very much doubted if Tom would be available to help the next day. Then, taking the plunge to get it over with, and looking him straight in the eye, she added, 'You can hardly expect him to, could you, after telling him that his precious plants were legally your property and he was not to move them without your permission. He was naturally very upset, and so was I when he told me.'

'Oh that!' Gerald gave a little laugh. 'I only said it to show him who was boss after he'd obviously been sponging on your good nature to help him out. I resented you being used, that's all, and he can take his plants away so long as he does so in his own time. And I hope you'll soon see you've made a mistake in letting him use your land.'

Anne, wanting to be sure of her ground, pushed back a retort she felt strongly inclined to make. But her hesitation encouraged Gerald to continue in the hope that at last he was regaining the upper hand.

'Perhaps it's natural,' he said ponderously, 'that ownership of a farm should have – er – gone to your head somewhat. Lack of management experience tempted you to lose a sense of fitness – to be indiscreet, and do things you would regret when mistakes became evident. Had you confided in me at the beginning I could have guided you, but for some reason I could never fathom you were intent on going it alone. And now you're landing yourself with problems you'll never be able to cope with. You women just aren't practical enough in such matters. Do I make myself clear Anne? I've no wish to be hurtful or critical, believe me.'

After a pause Anne said icily, 'Have you finished?'

Gerald blinked. 'You're not resentful are you?' he asked in surprise.

'Are you telling me,' she went on, 'that I'm not fit to be in charge of my own farm? You've admitted to winkling out of Tom that I'd allow him to have his plants there – after I told you that I'd explain when I was ready to do so. But because you've interfered and even threatened to claim those plants as your own on a trumped up pretext, I decided to act. They're all in my land now Gerald, and I helped Tom to move them. So now what?'

'I see it as more evidence,' Gerald growled, 'of your disloyalty and I can't condone it any more than I can condone your secrecy. And if he took time off to do the moving then I shall expect him to make it up to me over the weekend.'

'With my help,' Anne chuckled, 'it was all done after working hours. But that's not the only reason why I did so. I may as well tell you now that I'm going to back him in the nursery he's longing to set up –'

'What do you mean by that?' Gerald interrupted sharply.

'Believe it or not, Gerald,' Anne said calmly, 'I'm prepared to finance him and it won't be a sleeping partnership – in any sense. The idea of having a little part of the farm as a nursery for uncommon plants intrigues me and I know I'll enjoy learning about them and finding ways and means of selling them. Tom trusts me and I trust him, but I may have a partnership agreement drawn up. You've treated me all these years as if I could only function with your – guidance, you'd call it. But now I've discovered I've got some potential of my own I'm darn well going to develop it. And by the way, I've no intention of leaving you or causing a split in the family. This'll still be my base, unless of course you decide to kick me out.'

Gerald glowered as he stood up and poured out a whisky and soda. 'You must be mad! What you've just said is utter rubbish from what can only be a deranged mind. If you were to carry out such a ridiculous idea, it can do no other than cause the family split you've begun to widen further. It would completely undermine our position, socially – yours as well as mine – and the distraction would certainly spoil your relationship with Julian and Susan. You'd better think again Anne if you're capable of thinking rationally at all – which I doubt.'

It did not occur to Gerald as he lay fuming in bed that night that his own thoughts were somewhat irrational. His anger was charged with frustration because he could see no way of bringing Anne to her senses. He had accused her of madness, not that as a calculated threat to his own ideals it would stand up, but he believed he had full justification in whatever accusations he used to deflect her. What he'd said had sprung from the new and chilling fear that he now had very few options left. She seemed to be as impervious to entreaties and his chagrin had reached such a pitch that not even the pleasantries he'd enjoyed with Charlotte during the last three days offset his distress. Until a few weeks ago he'd felt so secure, so capable of manipulating anyone, including Anne. He had striven since schooldays to lay unshakeable foundations to an ordered, exemplary life in keeping with traditional values and ideals, and it was the woman he had chosen to share that life with him, along with its many benefits, who was hell bent on shattering all that. It wasn't madness, but an eruption of sheer, callous selfishness which her legacy had allowed to emerge. His thoughts went back in time to lay blame on her brother for being such a careless car driver and her father for switching the legacy to Anne. It would have been far better to have ensured that the farm be sold, with a big slice of the proceeds coming to her. That would have kept them together, but now the future was bleak – except for his new relationship with Charlotte.

There might still be ways, he pondered, which his vigilance would reveal, to retaliate, to make his prediction of her regret and failure a reality. Direct opposition would do no good, nor would he try to undermine her self confidence. This was something she'd often lacked in their early days together and he'd helped her over it. Now it had erupted in a totally new and dangerous shape flourishing, it seemed, on his opposition to it. Somehow it must be defeated but he could think of only two other means which might succeed, risky though they were. It was not in Gerald's nature to take risks, but needs must when the devil drives.

He had expected Anne to opt out of helping both in the Saturday preparations and the Sunday opening. This would have put a heavy burden on him, but would give him the opportunity of showing his contempt for her lapse. Anne's offer to help out as usual took him by surprise until it occurred to him that she might have deliberately avoided giving him cause for complaint. By enlisting other helpers, including Geoff and Doreen in occupation of the service flat, all was laid on for the visitors by opening time next day.

Never before, Gerald mused, had so much been done by so few in such a short time. And never had there been a display of colour to equal this last opening of the year. The dahlias, chrysanthemums, zinnias, geraniums and begonias had never been better, thanks to ample waterings during the drought. He was pleased with the way young Trevor took over Tom's duty at the plant stall. Not that there was very much to sell in mid-September, but with a new head gardener to take charge he would see to it that Trevor and Michael were encouraged to further his plans to have much more to offer next year. And he'd already resolved to increase public openings to the first Sunday in every month from April to October. The demand was there, judging by the attendance and takings, and it gave him a good feeling to be a benefactor to charitable causes as the owner of a unique private garden.

Gerald was, however, aware of a peculiar ambivalence in his attitude towards Anne. His antipathy towards her new interests, and especially to her association with Tom Berkeley, was in conflict with his thoughts on Charlotte Norton. He had toyed with the idea of inviting Charlotte for a weekend whilst the garden was still colourful. It would have been a good idea if he were sure it would evoke some jealousy in Anne, but the chances were that it might have the opposite effect, whilst laying him open to the charge of being two-faced. So long as Anne knew nothing of his friendship with Charlotte, right was all on his side. It was a slippery path, Gerald realised, that he was obliged to tread.

Another successful Open Sunday brought a resolve to drop his antagonism towards Tom. It had reached a peak point when Tom told him that Shirley had left him. This had brought an added fear that Anne had been more than sympathetic towards Tom, and resulted in his use of futile threats over the ownership of plants on his land.

Tom came to work as usual on the Monday morning, with no trace of shame on his face, but with a slight twinkle in his eye as he apologised for having taken his plants away without Gerald's permission.

'Oh – forget it Berkeley,' Gerald said in what was to Tom a surprisingly friendly tone. 'I'm not going to make an issue of it, Let's put it down to a misunderstanding. It did seem to me at one time you'd taken on the job here as a stop-gap, when I found out how concerned you were with the kind of plants which could not fit in with my style of gardening. Now that you're about to leave I can but wish you well, but you will leave the cottage clean and tidy, won't you?'

'Of course sir,' Tom replied, amazed.

Gerald gave him a wry, deprecating smile. 'Can I give you a piece of friendly advice to keep under your hat? – although I don't think I've ever seen you wearing one – but you know what I mean.'

Tom nodded expectantly.

'I believe my wife has offered to back your venture financially,' Gerald went on speaking softly. 'But I must warn you that you shouldn't bank on it, not as a long term thing. She's a very kind-hearted person, but she has what I can only see as a weakness for getting all excited over some do-good cause and then, suddenly, after a time, she loses all interest. This has happened several times in the twenty odd years we've been together and mostly I've had to sort of bale her out. More than once it's been pretty embarrassing. My guess is that you feel that you can trust her implicitly at this stage. Right, Tom?'

Disarmed somewhat by Gerald's use of his first name, Tom answered 'Well, yes, I've no reason not to trust her,' wincing inside.

'So have others, but since the Dunsford farm has been hers, she's acted very strangely. The reason being no doubt that she now has more opportunity to indulge in her whim. What I'm very much afraid of is that you'll be left stranded just when you thought success was coming at last. And of course the more she helps you, whether it's physical or financial, the more certain it is she'll suddenly tire of it, and the harder it will hit you. You may be thinking it's no concern of mine and let both you and her take the consequences, but since last week when I was so annoyed with you, I've realised I was rather hard on you. You've probably had more than your share of trouble and disappointment in life, and if I said nothing now, I'd have it on my conscience when you find you've been let down again.'

Tom's spirits had fallen. The old feeling of a trap closing in was coming over him once more.

'It hasn't been easy for me to tell you this Tom, but I had to do it. Have you any idea of the extent she's willing to back you – financially I mean? Not that I'd accuse her of any kind of trickery, but I do know that until her father died any money she had came from me. Even now she cannot have very much to play with.'

'She didn't mention a figure,' Tom said glumly, 'but she was willing to invest in more varieties and pay for a shed and a glasshouse for propagating.'

'Hm!' mused Gerald. 'I don't know what that would amount to – a thousand pounds at least, I'd guess, wouldn't you say?'

'Maybe.' Tom's thoughts went back to Anne's offer of a partnership agreement which was comforting if he could hold her to it.

Gerald turned away and began walking slowly along the garden path with head down as if deep in thought. Then turning back he smiled. 'Listen Tom, I see only one way out of what will be a disaster for you, and loss to my wife. I'd rather, much rather, fork out now than when the inevitable happens. I'm willing to pay you two thousand pounds if you'll undertake to move your plants within a month. And I'll undertake to find you a place to take them, where you can set up your nursery with a far better chance of success than you'd have around here.'

Tom, stuck for words, gave Gerald a wide-eyed stare. 'I – I just don't know what to say,' he muttered.

'No need to say anything Tom. But just think it over between now and when I go back to London tomorrow morning, when I'll expect an answer. It's your future that's at stake and what I've offered is a golden opportunity to stand on your own two feet – to be independent. Surely at your time of life after the rough passage you've had, that's what you want isn't it?'

For several weeks Gerald had seen Tom as rather contemptible, both as a man, as a gardener and to some extent as a threat because of Anne's interest in him. But now, as Tom wilted from the new line of attack, he began to feel a twinge of pity for him.

Coming closer, he tapped Tom's shoulder and said in a low, earnest voice, 'I'm a man of the world Tom and have a pretty good knowledge of human nature. My guess is that you've had a lot of frustration and have never had a partner or friend to give you the kind of advice and encouragement you needed. You probably made an unlucky marriage and now your wife has left you, it may well add to your sense of failure. But I doubt if that was your fault. I guess you're a soft touch where women are concerned and give in to their whims and notions for the sake of peace. You have to stand on your own two feet – back your judgement and refuse to pander. You've got what it takes to be your own master and forge ahead if only you'll let it come out. Be a man, Tom! Be yourself! Make your mind be as strong as your body. You are a strong man, but you only pretend you're not because you've let things happen just like most women do, instead of taking life as a challenge – like a man should. My offer is your golden opportunity, if you have the guts to take it.'

Chapter Twelve

A few months later the old Dunsford vicarage had been sold to an antique dealer, and the new one was at last taking shape. Anne had spotted Peter and Claire Hemming on the site one evening as she went back to Melthorpe. Joining them as they picked their way between what were to be rooms, it was Peter who reminded her that it was almost a year ago when they first met.

'I'll never forget,' he laughed, 'the look on your face when I came across you dabbling your feet from that crazy old bridge.'

'Tell me your version Anne,' Claire suggested. She'd only had Peter's and it made her think how she would have felt in Anne's predicament.

As good friends, they all three ended in laughing, till Peter remarked that had it not been for that first unorthodox introduction they would probably not be surveying what was, in a few weeks' time, to be their home.

'I just hope we'll be in residence by the time our baby comes,' Claire said anxiously. 'I wouldn't like to inflict nappies and howlings on your mother.'

'But she's going to miss your company anyway, and I'm not at all sure if she'll want to stay there alone. We can but wait and see. She'll make up her mind in her own good time and it's not for me to persuade her one way or the other.'

The delay on the part of the Ecclesiastical Commissioners, which Peter had seen as a threat to his staying on as vicar for the three parishes was, he learned, due to the obscure ownership of the plot on which the house was now being built. It was quite close to the church and had been let for years as an allotment type of garden for the sexton. It was when out of curiosity Peter had rummaged through an old chest in the vestry that the deeds were found, proving the plot to be church property acquired for an expected extension to the churchyard which, due to the reduced population of the village in the late 1800s was never required. In recent years it had become derelict with docks, ragwort and brambles and Peter feared it would be his responsibility to bring it back to a garden. 'I'm no gardener,' he remarked ruefully, at which Anne offered to send in a tractor and a rotavator when the builders had finished. 'I'll bless you for that Anne, but I still won't have much incentive to make it into a garden, and with Claire likely to be short of free time, the chances are that it will be grassed down ready for the next incumbent.'

'Oh dear,' Anne said, 'does that mean you'll be moving back to a town parish – or what?'

'It means, more likely I'll be kicked out. You see, I'm writing a book on how the Church is out of touch as a result of being bogged down by doctrines which have no validity. The so-called early church fathers made them as rules to ensure obedience to a priestly hierarchy which I'm quite sure Jesus never intended. Now that people have freed themselves from fear of hell-fire, the Church has got to go back to basic Christianity or it will fizzle out as archaic nonsense. And if my book gets published, it will probably make my job as a parson untenable. As it is, I feel I'm a hypocrite for having to preach or say what I don't really believe, and the few faithful around here don't like my watered down approach – including your own mother, Anne.'

Anne had been to church two or three times in the past year, and although not deeply stirred, had found Peter's sermons quite refreshing. Her mother had, she knew, been somewhat torn between her affection for Peter and Claire as companions sharing her house, and his earthy views on religion which emerged during the services she attended.

Claire was sitting down on a pile of bricks wearing a faintly amused expression. Responding to the glance Anne gave her she said, 'I s'pose it's a case of a man's got to do what a man's got to do. I don't think it will come to Peter being unfrocked as they call it. I agree with him most of the way and I'll stick by him all the way wherever it leads. He knows that – don't you Peter?'

Peter nodded with a grateful smile. Then looking at Anne he spoke of the hints her mother had made recently that she must soon be looking out for somewhere else to live. 'I thought perhaps you knew – until you said just now that she'd decide in her own good time. Quite frankly, I think she's decided that when we move she'll move out too.'

Anne said she was aware of this as a strong possibility. 'But,' she went on, 'I'm in a difficult position because I don't think she approves of me spending more time helping in Tom's nursery than I do back at Melthorpe. She's afraid of what people might think and believes it's my duty towards Gerald to be there even though he's away at least half the week. The plain fact is, I s'pose, that I've become so interested in Tom's venture that it's opened up a whole new dimension for me. At Melthorpe I was just acting a part, giving me no satisfaction – not even as a caretaker with a couple living in the flat. I go back now every evening tired but content because I feel I've done some useful work here in Dunsford. Head full of plant names, and not very good company for Gerald when he's home. He goes to his study and I get stuck into a book after we've eaten. Julian and Susan are seldom home, and Susan at least says it's my right to choose what I do with my life. Am I supposed to vegetate because Gerald and mother – and maybe Julian – think I'm becoming a tear-away?'

It was the first time Anne had confided her feelings to anyone but Susan, although even she had a few reservations on the score of propriety. Her involvement with Tom Berkeley would have been brief but for her Dunsford farm legacy.

Nowadays Tom's anxieties did not often surface. At Melthorpe last year they were seldom absent, but the man most responsible for them had unwittingly been the one to dispel those affecting his future. Shirley's departure had cleared his mind of one major worry leaving the way open to take up Anne's offer with no reservations other than his undermined faith in himself. Gerald had demanded an answer to his offer in a matter of hours, but in less than one hour Tom had made up his mind to turn it down. To couple what at first appeared as a generous offer with a tirade on Tom's shortcomings as a man had been a gambler's throw. Nor did Gerald's overt reference to Anne's propensity for short-lived enthusiasm match up with what else he said. At first this had bothered him with the fear that those allegations might be true. But what came out of that uncomfortable final confrontation with Gerald was a growing sense of his own importance. Some of Gerald's remarks about his lack of spirit had been true, and had goaded him into taking a more positive attitude, which in turn began a process of coming to terms with himself. Bogged down as he had been for years by pressures from outside – including Shirley – and from inside due to his sense of guilt and failure, now there were bright rays of hope and resolve to be seen and pursued. Until then Tom had seen Anne as a kindly, sympathetic person who had taken pity on him, realising belatedly that she too had personal problems.

Such thoughts had been hatching in Tom's mind during that week when Anne helped him move his plants to Dunsford. Then, as he met Gerald coming to find him again just before he left for London, every shadow of doubt vanished.

'Well, Berkeley?' Gerald had said with as much of a leer as a grin. 'Have you seen sense yet – about my offer?'

'Yes major,' Tom had replied firmly, using the title he had come to despise.

'Then what's your answer. No ifs or buts. Plain yes or no.'

'It's definitely no,' Tom smiled calmly. 'I'll leave the cottage spick and span whenever you wish me to go. And I hope you'll take to your next gardener better than you took to me.'

Gerald shot him a glance with eyebrows raised in surprise, and he turned and marched away swinging his arms soldier fashion, which had struck Tom as rather odd.

Anne had found Tom in the garden next morning. She had heard him softly whistling to himself behind the high yew hedge as he planted a new bed of strawberries. His broad smile had made her ask if he'd had some good news.

'Not exactly,' he'd said. 'It's just that I've suddenly begun to see things differently. Got rid of some inhibitions, you could say.'

'I'm glad, Tom. But how come?'

'Well, the major gave me some friendly advice yesterday and it stuck. He didn't mince his words and they stung at first. But after he'd gone it dawned on me that he'd been spot on, and it was up to me to come to terms with myself – warts an'all.'

'What he said, and the way he said it,' Tom had added, 'has somehow taken quite a load off my mind, and I hope it eases yours too Anne.'

It was not only Anne's sense of freedom which ruled out any possibility of going back to her old life. Nor was it entirely her enthusiasm for the nursery venture which enticed her along the path she had taken. Her interest in plants had increased as growth and variety had expanded, along with her financial commitment. Tom had bought in with her money ten each of over a hundred kinds of perennials from various specialist nurseries. She had also paid for a glasshouse for propagating, along with a shed and shade cover, pots and plant trays, peat, sand and various needful pieces of equipment, together with a second-hand Ford Transit van. In total these cost over two thousand pounds and now, any day, a firm of well sinkers was due to come to drill for a water supply for irrigating both farm and nursery. From the cramped plots filled with plants last year at Melthorpe, the odd shaped field at Dunsford was colouring up with over an acre of plants which she had helped to produce.

Along with other incentives to carry on was Tom himself. The change in his manner and outlook since he left Melthorpe to lodge with Mabel Adams had been quite remarkable, though she held back from remarking upon it. He told her no more of that last encounter with Gerald which had sparked off such a change in him, and Anne had not probed further. But within a matter of days Tom had become more decisive, more cheerful and zestful as if all his frustrations and sense of failure had vanished. He had insisted that he could cope with autumn planting in his spare time, whilst Ted Fletcher needed him for farm work. For a few weeks it was Anne who cared for the plants, heeling some temporarily and dividing others for Tom to plant at weekends, now that two acres of the cole seed rape had been ploughed under.

It was plant propagation which aroused Anne's interest so profoundly. And it was Tom's own feel for plants which, as he showed her how to acquire it, made her estimation of him and his skill and knowledge change her attitude towards him from one of pity to something akin to admiration. Where certain kinds responded to division he taught her how to feel with fingers and thumbs where resistance to division was least. A knife, he explained, should only be used when fingers failed, since forcing in the blade would leave a raw wound, whereas a gentle but firm teasing apart was likely to produce better results and a greater increase. There were other propagating skills which she lapped up. How to deal with the fibrous roots of phlox and Japanese anemones which produced new little plants from tiny eye buds, to chunky pieces of fleshy rooted verbascums and oriental poppies which grew from making new shoots so long as they were inserted the right way up. Green cuttings, Anne learned, included the vernal shoots from the base of the plant, and these needed a different technique from tips of more mature growth. In both cases timing was a vital factor as was after-care in watering or shading from strong sunlight.

Seed sowing of subjects which would come true was another area where much was to be learned. Tom had saved seeds of several from last year's laid in plants, and although he gave Anne a run-down on how and when to sow, he elected to do the sowing himself. 'You've enough to learn and do with cuttings and division for this season,' he told her with a glint in his eyes she'd never seen whilst he was at Melthorpe. This, she'd found was true enough during the first spring time at Dunsford, and as each kind of plant was dealt with, she recorded it in a notebook for future reference, which was of special interest when a batch of cuttings became rooted and ready for potting and planting.

When the lighter evenings came, as well as on Saturdays and Sundays, Tom liked to have batches ready for him to plant in the open field, since during the week he was on farm work under Ted Fletcher's direction. All three were aware that before long farm work would have to take second place as the nursery expanded. And by common consent it was decided that no effort should be made until next year to sell what they produced.

It was Anne who came up with this suggestion. It made sense to her to concentrate first and foremost on building up stocks in both quantity and variety before offering any for sale. Hers was almost the sole financial backing, and although Tom sometimes showed concern at how deeply she had become involved, with anxiety about a return for her investment, she had no doubts on the rightness of her policy.

'No need for you to worry Tom,' she said gaily. 'I'm certain we're on the right lines. From what I've read and gathered here and there there's quite a boom in perennials – or they're coming into their own maybe, and it's the less common kinds that are most in demand. Anybody can produce lupins, delphiniums, michaelmas daisies and such like cheaply, but we're out to cater for a more up-market trade, aren't we?'

'You're right, of course,' Tom agreed. 'But it has to be mail order. A catalogue will be another expense before you get any orders to pay for it – together with everything else you've paid for.'

And now, nine months later, Tom and Anne were partners in a project of absorbing mutual interest and Gerald's name was scarcely ever mentioned.

Chapter Thirteen

Not much traffic used the road flanking the new nursery. It linked Dunsford and Baldisham and was quite narrow, but with the field gently sloping away towards the little river, passers-by could see the flowers over the low hedge and some cars slowed down. During July, curiosity had been aroused by the tall drilling rig, but the operators discouraged anyone who came close to watch the proceedings.

Six inch diameter steel tubes were hammered in by a weight dropped from the top of the rig, and as a boring tool inside the tube brought up the soil, so the tubes were pushed down. First came up a subsoil of sand, which at eight feet turned into a stony mixture of sand and clay. Then came grey-green clay, with occasional flints for the next forty feet. The operator explained that one could never tell how deep one had to go before reaching the water-bearing chalk, nor how far into the chalk they would need to penetrate before picking up one of the underground streams of water. The deeper they had to go, the greater would be the cost of the job.

Through the day water had to be poured in to make drilling easier. Then, when the chalk came up at sixty five feet, the work became easier and another sixty feet brought a grin from the crew as the white soupy stuff appeared. After that came the pumping process. At first the pump spewed out a white emulsion type liquid into a trench to lead it away from the site. After four hours it was like adulterated milk, and then similar to glacier water, till at last it came clear. And when it was almost dark, after fourteen hours, the pump was switched off. The operator invited Anne and Tom to peer down the tube, aided by a torch. There was a glint of water only a few feet down and it was rising. Slowly it reached within a foot of the top of the tube which itself was only just below the land surface.

'It's a good head,' the man said casually. 'You'll never be short of water however much you take out.'

'It's magic!' Anne exclaimed. 'And I'm going to sample it, if any of you have a cup to drink from.'

Amused, the operator offered the cup lid of his flask, and Anne and Tom drank in turn and smacked their lips as if it were champagne, 'Beats tap water,' Tom said, whilst Anne remarked on how cold it was. But both knew that the purpose for which their artesian well had been made would have to wait. To install a pump, lay irrigation mains for use when crops needed it would cost even more than the well. Anne had seen danger ahead with her savings almost exhausted and the farm account at the bank showing only enough credit to cover wages and other expenses until after the harvest. Fortunately rains had avoided the need for irrigation this year, but droughts would come again. 'All being well,' she told Tom, 'we'll have it fixed up by next spring.' But only she knew that in all probability she would have to raise a large sum to provide another home for her mother. Tom would have worried had she told him.

Anne's ownership of the farm had changed her attitude to money. Before, she had saved and invested as if she needed the security for the future. This alone had given her a slight feeling of independence, although the money came from Gerald. But since owning the farm and especially since going into business with Tom, she had gladly and freely spent as a worthwhile investment, giving her the chance to be expansive in more ways than one. The new well had been booked as a contract job after having completed the formalities required to obtain a licence. This the operator had done on her behalf, and although she was aware of funds running low, she hadn't the heart to hold back once the licence came, and the nursery watering would have to rely for a time on the present extension of the public mains.

Anne had drifted blithely along, too absorbed with the new venture to give more than an occasional thought to the clause in her father's will, with its obligation to provide a home for her mother. She knew that there were investments made to yield an income on which her mother could live, but she had forgotten what these amounted to. And another house hadn't appeared to matter greatly whilst Eileen was content to live in the farmhouse.

Soon after meeting the Hemmings on the site of the new vicarage, Anne had put the question as diplomatically as she could. Her mother had become increasingly touchy and Anne knew that stemmed from her own partial escape from Gerald, coupled with her association with Tom. 'I've been wondering,' Eileen said coldly, 'whether you intended treating me as you have your husband.'

Anne was tempted to try once more to explain. But Eileen would only remain frigid in her belief that Anne had forsaken her clear duty to follow a hair-brained course and put her family to shame. None of her excuses would be valid.

'I'll not neglect my duty to you mother,' Anne told her. 'I've always said I'll carry out the terms of Dad's will if you move into a smaller house – wherever you choose it to be. I've fancied you'd prefer a cosy little house nearby and I quite think we get planning permission on our land. But it's entirely your choice, even if you prefer to stay here with someone else to take the Hemmings' place when they move out.'

Eileen stiffened and sniffed. 'I've no wish to stay here. And don't you realise that people are talking about you and that man Berkeley, asking pointed questions? The pair of you are making it impossible for me to live here or anywhere in Dunsford. You seem to have lost all sense of propriety, as well as duty. It makes me so ashamed and I can't condone or find excuses for you. If I'd thought for a moment that you'd have done such a thing, I would never have agreed when your Dad suggested leaving the farm to you in his will. No more would he. And doesn't that touch you, knowing that what you're doing would be dead against his wishes?'

'I'm not doing anything wrong, mother. And the farm's in good shape. After all, the nursery is only a sideline.'

'It's wrong to neglect your family and it's wrong to spend so much time away from where you belong. And it's wrong to spend so much time and money on another man. I've decided I'd like to move to Attleborough. Gerald's mother has written to say that there's a house for sale next door to her, and Gerald has offered to do what you should have done – take me to see it on Friday.'

'I'm sorry mother,' Anne said hiding what she felt. 'Obviously I should have spoken openly sooner, but didn't want to influence what had to be your own decision.'

'That's as may be Anne, and if you're about to offer to come too on Saturday, I can tell you it won't be necessary. As you've just said, it has to be my own decision. You've chosen to ignore the welfare of your family and must take the consequences.'

Trembling with suppressed emotions, Anne made one more mild

protest against Eileen's uncompromising attitude and for an hour vented her feelings on weeds in a stock bed on the nursery. Matters were, she realised, coming to a head. Till now she had shied away from what she knew at heart must come to a confrontation. She did not and could not expect Gerald to accept the situation as it stood. Nor could she really blame him if he decided on a showdown. In following her own inclinations it was up to him rather than herself to make the next move, and she was quite content to let the drifting continue. Gerald had begun to take the initiative again after months of seeming quiescence, and as she snatched out groundsel and shepherd's purse, she tried to guess what his next move would be.

Anne's thoughts settled on Julian and Susan. They were both due to come home in a week's time. Julian was to join Wroxley, Ross and Partners after a spell in Sweden studying modern forestry techniques. Susan had decided to study Baroque Roccoco for a time and was due to go to Paris.

When Gerald returned from London on the Thursday he told Anne that he was taking her mother the following morning to view a vacant house in Attleborough. 'I don't suppose,' he said, 'you'll consider it necessary to come too, even though it will be up to you to fork out if it's suitable. I think it will be, and she'll have a good neighbour with my mother next door. It will then be up to you to come to terms with the agents.'

'Very well,' Anne said brightly, adding that Eileen had already spoken of the prospect and that she was quite prepared to do what was necessary.

'It's also necessary.' Gerald continued with a cold look in his eyes, 'to put Julian and Susan fully in the picture. You must be blind or besotted if you think you can continue blithely oblivious to your family obligations. I've put up with a hell of a lot from your – incalcitrance, and it can't go on. Do you understand? It must stop. Is that clear?

Anne nodded with a wry smile. 'You must do as you think best Gerald. If you're going to Attleborough in the morning, I'll take a look at the property in the afternoon. I need to do some shopping and can call and see the agents if mother likes the house.'

If Gerald wished to adopt a cold, business-like approach, that was all to the good. She could do likewise, but what she'd already begun to dread was a family conference at which emotions would be hard if not impossible to keep under control. Inevitably the blame would descend on her shoulders and although she believed she could hold out against Gerald and Julian, Susan's attitude might be decisive. She had no stomach for hitting back at Gerald as being the cause of her desperate bid for freedom, nor for her mother's presence at lunch after they returned from viewing the Attleborough house. The fact that Gerald had invited her to lunch without telling Anne was, she believed, another of his ploys.

'Did the house appeal to you mother?' Anne asked brightly on their return.

Eileen, avoiding a direct answer, said it didn't matter whether she liked it or not because the price would probably rule out any possibility of going there to live, nice though it would be to have Mrs Potts senior as a next door neighbour. Then she added, 'She was quite shocked to learn how things stood. Gerald hadn't told her – too ashamed no doubt – but I thought she ought to know. You'd be wise not to call in if you go to see the house.'

Gerald joined them. 'Talking about the house are you?'

'Yes,' Anne said. 'But although I gather it would suit, no price has been mentioned. Still, I can find out when I go this afternoon, if you'd rather not tell me. And I'll be seeing the bank manager too. He knows all about the investments Dad made.'

Gerald snorted. 'This'll come as a shock, but I may as well tell you. It's thirty-nine thousand, five hundred, for exactly the same size and design as my mother's, which cost three and a half in 1952.' Anne pretended not to be shocked. She was well aware that prices had soared but had fondly imagined what she knew to be a two-bedroomed bungalow would be no more than thirty thousand, even though it was in a select part of the little town. 'Well – we'll see what can be done, won't we?'

'I don't think that "we" comes into it,' Gerald persisted. 'And my guess is that the bank will give you the same advice as I gave you over a year ago. Remember? When I said you'd do well to sell the Dunsford house separately. Now's your chance. But you'd find yourself rather stuck if you decided to be done with the farm as well – after what you've spent on it for no good purpose.'

Anne merely said, 'Point taken Gerald.'

'And it will need redecorating Anne,' Eileen said as Gerald drew back a chair for her at the lunch table.

Two hours later Mr Palmer, the bank manager, was going through the investment documents one by one, making notes as he did so, whilst Anne sat tensely waiting for the final figure. 'Well short of forty thousand I fear Mrs Potts. About thirty-five I make it, but they're pretty sound, especially the Halifax. I've no doubt they would fix you up with a mortgage, but as I expect you know, the interest on all these has gone into your mother's account as her income under your father's will, and if –'

'I see what you're getting at Mr Palmer,' Anne interrupted. 'Mother has some money of her own, but I'd rather not ask her how much – and well –isn't there some other way, so as to let her keep things as they are? My husband suggested I sold the farmhouse. But what would you advise? I certainly don't intend selling the farm itself.'

'My advice Mrs Potts,' he smiled broadly over his glasses, 'is to let the bank lend you the money. I think it would be a big mistake to sell the house away from the farm, when as a holding it offers more than ample security. If you have no tenant for the house when your mother vacates it, you could let it – at a rent, very likely, which would cover our charges for the loan. I won't call it a mortgage because a bank loan allows you to reduce it whenever your profits from the farm allow. And it's still profitable under your ownership. I think you are to be congratulated, I really do.'

Anne warmed towards Mr Palmer enough to tell him about her nursery venture and how, next year all being well, she expected to see some worthwhile return from the outlay. He commended her intention of making and keeping the farm and nursery accounts separate. She also explained the part Tom was playing and how his wages, as from when he became full-time in the nursery, would have to be paid from a separate bank account.

'I'd like you to come and see what we are doing Mr Palmer,' she said, after he'd assured her that she could feel free to purchase the house for her mother.

'And I'll be one of your first customers, Mrs Potts. My garden needs more variety. I'm getting tired of bedding out twice a year.'

'Well, did you look over the house?' Gerald asked in a casual way over tea.

Anne, feeling bubbly inside at her successful afternoon, was half inclined to tease him, but then decided to play it straight. 'No,' she drawled. 'You and mother did so and that's all that matters. I expect she'll want to go again to decide what colour schemes she wants when it's redecorated. I'll phone her after tea.'

'You – you mean you've agreed to purchase?'

'Uha!' Anne smiled. 'If no snags crop up it should be all ready by the time the Hemmings leave her.'

Gerald probed but Anne saw no reason to go into detail on how the deal was arranged.

'Have it your own way,' he growled as he drank his tea, making cup and saucer clatter when he'd finished.

Softening a little as he left her, she thanked him for taking Eileen to view the bungalow and said she was perfectly willing to take her next time. Then she dialled Eileen. 'I hope you haven't changed your mind, mother,' she said breezily. 'Because the deal's been done and you just say when you're ready for me to take you over again to decide on decorating.'

Eileen made an effort to thank her. Then came reminders that there was no point in going over until all was signed up and that she could not leave Dunsford until the Hemmings had moved into the new vicarage. And that she had to decide what to do with the surplus furniture. 'You've been very hasty Anne,' she said with more deliberation. 'I think I've a right to know that it's all above board – how much you agreed to pay and where the money is coming from – and such like. Did you pay the full price?'

'Not quite. I managed to knock off enough to pay the cost of redecorating, that's all. Tell you more when I see you.'

Anne's elation did not last many days as she reminded herself that when Julian and Susan came home Gerald might well use them to put pressure on her where he had failed. Her own intentions as well as her knowledge of Gerald indicated that matters were coming to a head, and there was no way of avoiding it. She could not expect him to take no further action. She had not neglected what she considered her essential duties at Melthorpe and was willing to continue performing them as she'd done for the past year or more, although Gerald's view was obviously very different. So much depended on whose part Susan took when it came to a showdown. And as Anne's thoughts centred more on Susan she began to realise that she was the only person to restrain her from leaving Gerald and Melthorpe.

Gerald joined her, as he mostly did when at home, in watching the 9 o'clock television news. Sometimes they both stayed in to see a comedy programme before one or other went to their own room. Gerald had noticed the change which came over her during the evening and just as she was about to leave the lounge he gave her a quizzical look. 'Having second thoughts Anne?' he asked. 'Not surprising I s'pose after doing such a hasty deal over the house.'

'Just a headache,' Anne replied, blinking her eyelids and yawning. 'Goodnight – see you in the morning,' she added to avoid further questioning.

It had become a regular thing on calm, summer nights to lean her arms on the window sill before undressing. More often than not Tibbles climbed up the wistaria to join her. Her cat did not come until she'd got undressed and drawn on her night-gown. Then, with her thick hair combed and brushed, she settled down in bed, easing Tibbles off her chest so that she could read her book. Half an hour later Anne was just about to switch off the bedside light when she heard the bedroom door handle creak. The door opened enough to make her sit bolt upright. 'Who is it?' she called out.

'It's only me,' Gerald said softly as he filled the widening gap.

'What do you want?'

'Can't you guess Anne?' he said, making as if to unbelt his gaudy dressing gown to reveal his naked body. Tibbles took fright and disappeared out of the window. 'What I want,' Gerald went on in a loud whisper, 'is what's known as conjugal rights. It's over two years since you went frigid on me – but you're different now aren't you?'

Taking no chances Anne slid swiftly out of the opposite side of her bed and grabbing her dressing gown made for her bathroom door. Then with a safe distance between her and Gerald she turned round with eyes blazing, belying her smile. 'You look quite ridiculous Gerald,' she hissed. 'Whatever your motives, you should know better than to attempt rape, because I'll lock myself in my bathroom all night if need be. Do be sensible and go back to bed with a stiff whisky or something.'

'So be it,' he growled. 'Just another of my rights you've denied me, and from now on I'll put the screws on you.'

When Anne finally fell asleep, she'd found only one explanation which made sense. To approach her like that was so out of character that she had to conclude it was an act, a part of a plot he'd hatched up to confound her.

There was no reference to the incident from either Anne or Gerald at breakfast next morning. Conversation was at an all time low for the whole of the day, part of which Anne spent with her mother, with time to spare to chat with Tom at work on the nursery, confining what she said to the work he had for her during the next few days.

Gerald left early on the Monday so as to be back when Julian and Susan arrived, which Anne saw as somewhat ominous. As well she might, for within hours of their arrival, Julian on Thursday and Susan on Friday, Anne knew that he'd had private talks with each of them. Though never demonstrative, Julian's expression was austere when he cornered her. She decided to forestall him, since he was obviously ill at ease.

'You've come to tell me,' she said with a sympathetic smile, 'that I've let the family down, haven't you? I've no wish to cause you distress Julian, but my only excuse is that now you and Susan are adults, making your own way in life, I feel entitled to live the rest of my own life as I wish and not as others wish. Wouldn't you say I have this right?'

Julian shuffled uneasily avoiding her eyes. 'I suppose so,' he muttered, 'at least in a way. But I'd have thought you could have made some compromise which wouldn't disrupt the family, instead of spending so much of your time at Dunsford, I mean. And be – more involved with Melthorpe. I think Dad's having a pretty raw deal.'

'Julian dear,' Anne sighed with soft intensity, 'I know this is what you must be thinking, but it would never have occurred to you that for years and years I stifled my own longings until last year when I realised what a raw deal I was having – as your father's shadow, or something similar. Now I know there's no room for compromise – on his part as well as mine. So, my dear, I'll just have to take what's coming to me – whatever that might be. That's all I can say, knowing I stand condemned – for wanting to be myself.'

It came as a relief to Anne that Susan appeared in less of a hurry to have it out with her, although she was fairly certain that Gerald had talked privately with her soon after she arrived. After two days at home, however, she said she supposed a private chat was called for.

Anne agreed. 'But first, do come and take a look at the nursery. Just the two of us, and if need be you can say what you have to there, rather than here.'

'Okay, but won't Tom want to show us around?'

'Not likely. They're all busy with silage cutting and carting.' As they walked the centre pathway between rows of plants all labelled with their botanic names, Anne was glad not only for suggesting this visit, but because Susan was so obviously interested. She explained that there were now about 300 different kinds altogether and what a joy it had been for her to do most of the propagating. In the little greenhouse and in outside frames there was batches of cuttings Anne had taken and cared for, and she unfolded her plans on how to offer these for sale next spring after taking stock of the quality and quantity required. And they sampled the water from the new artesian well before Susan sat down on a bale of peat and lit a cigarette.

'Oh my, oh my!' she said, 'I don't know what to say, except that in a peculiar way I envy you mother.'

'How come?'

'Just that you're so absorbed and so productive. And I'm older now than you were when you married, and having got a degree don't have much idea how I'm going to make use of it. What you're doing is what you always advised Julian and I to do – make our own choices in life and stand on our own two feet.'

There was a long silence and then Anne said wistfully, 'Once I got married I had no choice, Susan. Do you blame me for striking out when the chance came?'

'How can I? We're talking,' Susan reflected, 'as if a break-up is inevitable aren't we? But is it?'

Anne spread her hands with a look of resignation in her eyes. 'I can't go back to the old life, so I suppose –'

'Are you in love with Tom, mother?' Susan asked suddenly.

Anne blinked and then gave a little laugh. 'Not that I'm aware of. Tom's a very reserved man and so wedded to his plants that I don't think of him in any other way than a business partner I can respect – even if he isn't all that business-like sometimes.'

'I just wondered,' Susan continued. 'He's the bête noir in Dad's eyes – I expect you know – and while you're in close contact with him, then a break-up is inevitable. Does it worry you to think you'll be branded as the offending party if Dad goes for a divorce?'

Another hollow laugh from Anne. 'That would be the least of my worries. Which brings me back to the greatest – what would it do to you?'

Susan put an arm round Anne and gave her a kiss on her cheek. 'Don't let it worry you ma,' she whispered. 'It'll be better than the present state of play. I'll be all right, especially if you team up with Tom and live at the farm when Gran moves out – even if you're still only good business partners. And if I may come and stay with you sometimes I'd love to learn how to take cuttings and things.'

Anne's tears came swiftly. 'Oh Susan love, you don't know what you've done for me saying that.'

Chapter Fourteen

Neither Gerald nor Charlotte had found flat sharing entirely satisfactory. Both were aware of each other's short term problems and these were constantly at the back of their minds. For Charlotte it was the need of a new husband willing and able to fit in with her deep-seated longings for children first and a house in the country as a close second. For Gerald it was the worsening situation at Melthorpe due entirely to Anne's virtual rejection of all he'd done for her.

Gerald, in the first flush of his closer acquaintance with Charlotte had seen her as a replacement for Anne in London, with the remote possibility of eventually her taking over at Melthorpe too. Now that he'd begun divorce proceedings, this aspect had become uppermost in his mind. What bedevilled his thoughts were not so much whether or not she would accept him, but whether – if she did – he could match her strong personality. During their flat sharing there had been problems calling for compromises which went against the grain. He could do no other than agree to her having occasional male acquaintances in for an evening, leaving him to entertain himself. Nor did she take kindly to being seen in public with him lest people thought she was his mistress. He could but agree that in this sense her position was somewhat invidious, especially as she also resented being seen as little more than a housekeeper.

Gerald's admiration of Charlotte's poise, her intellect and aristocratic background was, however, in no way diminished. He realised now that he should have set his sights higher instead of choosing a yeoman farmer's daughter for a wife. A woman of Charlotte's calibre and social background would not have let herself – and him – down in favour of an employee. She might be less malleable than Anne, but he felt now that he could respect her views and wishes to a more tolerable degree if she became his wife and the mistress of Melthorpe.

There was no doubt in Gerald's mind that Charlotte would take to Melthorpe. But there was a doubt on the score of children. If he were to marry Charlotte, he would have to perform as a frequent duty what till now had been a somewhat rare pleasure, which Charlotte offered as a favour. It was one thing to feel still capable of performing at nearly sixty years of age, but could be quite another to be called upon to do so more or less on demand perhaps three or four times a week in order to make Charlotte pregnant.

Because he had so much on his mind he had all but turned down an invitation to spend a week in Scotland grouse shooting. Then on the last day of July he decided the break might be just what was needed. He had to know one way or another since he'd never given Charlotte the slightest hint of ever asking her to marry him, just as he'd led Anne to believe that he'd employed a part-time daily woman at the London flat. Now he'd got to put the vital question to Charlotte and because she would naturally want to see Melthorpe before he did so, he saw it as a good scheme to let her do so on her own whilst he was away in Scotland. It was tricky, nevertheless, because neither Anne nor Charlotte should suspect.

Before he left for Scotland on 10 August there was the monthly Open Sunday to arrange and attend. Stephen Perkins, the new gardener, had proved to be expert in producing extra plants for sale as well as keeping up the display beds to Gerald's standards. A five per cent bonus on Open Day sales had been a spur, but extra advertising had brought much more demand too than home produced plants, flowers and other produce could meet. The first Sunday in August proved to be so rewarding that, added to previous monthly openings, the donations to charities seemed certain to double last year's total by the end of the season. It was so simple and such a pleasure to benefit good causes, putting him in the clear by advertisements declaring, 'All proceeds are donated to Charities'.

Gerald was inclined to play down to Charlotte the scope and importance of these Open Sundays. He could not be quite sure of her full cooperation if she became the lady of the manor. She might resent the commercial aspects and it was best that she should see Melthorpe in its serenity alone.

'It's just occurred to me Charlotte,' he said before leaving for Scotland. 'If you have time to spare whilst I'm away, why not pop down to Melthorpe? It's looking pretty good just now and if I tell

Anne and Perkins to expect you as an old friend, you could bring back some fresh produce and flowers. And you could even use the excuse of going to Marlington too.'

'Sounds like a good idea,' Charlotte mused, keeping to herself the belief that Gerald had underestimated her own perspicacity.

'I can't guarantee that Anne will be there,' Gerald continued. 'Not that you'll need to see her. If she's at Dunsford, or otherwise absent, I'll leave word with the live-in servant just in case you want to go indoors for any reason. Can I tell them which day you'll be going?'

'Let's say Thursday,' Charlotte said, offering her cheek for a good-bye kiss. 'Have a good shoot and don't get shot,' she added flippantly.

Thursday came, dull and windy. Charlotte decided to drive straight to Marlington Hall. It was rather like visiting a family mausoleum, but at least it was still there, a little more unkempt than a year ago. She'd heard that it had been bought by a property developer but there was as yet no sign of development, whatever that could mean. The drive gates had been open but there were no signs, nothing. Charlotte would not have gone but for a reason she had thought up as an extension to Gerald's suggestion. Heading south again after eating her sandwiches she took the first turn off the main road which indicated the way to Dunsford. But Norfolk signposts were confusing for she arrived at Baldisham where no Dunsford sign was to be seen. 'Turn back and take the Melthorpe road and you'll pass through Dunsford first,' she was told.

It was the sight of flowers that made her stop and seeing a woman at work she drew in to the grass verge. 'Mrs Potts I believe? I'm Charlotte Norton.'

'Correct,' Anne said amiably. 'I understood you were going to Melthorpe today, but you've come from the opposite direction.'

This was the opening Charlotte had hoped for, so as to put Anne at ease. She explained that she'd taken a wrong turning having been to Marlington first. 'That's where I met your husband a year ago when the family estate came on the market. I met him again recently and he suggested calling to see Melthorpe Manor when I said I'd like to see the old place again. I hope I'm not intruding by calling here first. I'd heard about your nursery but scarcely expected to see it.'

In the next half hour Charlotte learned all she needed to know of Anne's nursery. 'Someday, maybe, I'll be asking for your catalogue, but I must confess that what I'm seeing here are nearly all strangers to me.'

Beguiled, Anne mentioned her ownership of the farm which had given her the opportunity, with the help of an expert in his spare time. She was somewhat intrigued by Charlotte's visit. Anne looked at her watch and then at Charlotte, who was stooping to read the plant names on labels. 'Adonis – that must be named after the Greek god. But the plants look dead.'

Anne explained that having flowered in February they were now dormant. 'It's nearly four o'clock,' she added, 'and I'm due to go back to Melthorpe for an hour or two. Would you care to come and have tea with me? You can then wander round the garden. The gardeners will have left something for you to take back with you.'

After tea in the lounge, Charlotte insisted on carrying a tray back to the kitchen. 'All very spic and span,' she remarked, 'and the flower beds are nothing if not colourful. Do visitors behave on what I hear are monthly Open Sundays for charity?'

And when at half past six Charlotte said she must be on her way back, Anne found herself saying she must come again before summer ended. There was something about Charlotte she liked – a friendly directness and seemingly wide interests. When she'd gone, Anne felt some regret for not asking for her address.

Back at Dunsford, Anne made excuses to Tom for being late. They had arranged to begin stocktaking now that a full assessment could be made of what would form the catalogue of plants for sale. On her clip board, Anne began to enter names as Tom gave her the numbers. He knew how many plants per twenty-yard row and what to allow for a few non survivors in each. With his superior knowledge of each kind's potential for ease or otherwise of propagation, he was the one to set a limit on the number available for sale. Then, having covered all the open ground stock and the few kinds grown in pots, back-up rooted cuttings and seedlings would also have to be recorded. After that they would have to be listed in alphabetical order, described and priced – a task which would take up many evenings in autumn to be in print by February.

After almost a year Tom was only just beginning to overcome his 'too good to be true' change in circumstances. His attitude to Anne as his benefactor had changed only because of her insistence that he had no cause to feel beholden to her. He had seen her as being remote from him in social standing after years of having to show respect for his betters. And even now, after her assurances, he found it difficult to talk freely on any subject which had no link with work. Recently he had begun to wonder if this was because of his own reluctance to be drawn, but he still found it hard to broach any other subject with her.

The books she had lent him had impressed him. The holistic approach to physical ailments made sense, but scarcely applied to him, fit as he was. But what he'd read about wholeness of personality and ways and means of coming to terms with one's psychological make-up also made sense. This was, he felt, his greatest need. But he was still at a loss to know how to set about it. It came as startling news to read, for example, that the human brain was in two compartments – one with masculine and the other with feminine orientation. He'd always imagined that sex and gender meant much the same thing, but to learn that each sex had an element of the other within them had been very disturbing to him. Even so, it became intriguing the more he thought about it, especially when he also discovered that the basic sex was female and that human embryos were programmed in their genes to become male several weeks after conception.

A year had passed since Shirley left him. He had decided to make sure she never came back by getting a divorce. The remaining furniture at the cottage had been sent to a collective auction at Watton, but the proceeds were too meagre to go very far towards his legal freedom. Sadly he lost touch with Sandra altogether and he had no idea where she was. His only contact with his family was by three or four letters a year and his agnosticism discouraged contact with the vicar, apart from which Anne's mother's disapproval of him left him more of a loner than ever.

But Tom was in both Mabel Adams' and Ted Fletcher's good books. Mabel could not have treated him better if he'd been the son she never had, and he enjoyed doing little jobs for her, including care of her garden which, because of her arthritic hip, Ted or his son had previously done for her. Ted was expert at good humoured banter but Geoff, his son who was the farm's leading tractor driver and ploughman, was of a dour and sometimes surly nature. The other farm workers, pigman, cowman and a happy-go-lucky lad treated him with tolerant amusement as a gardener out of his element, but with some disdain for his propensity for slogging. Ted

Fletcher once slyly remarked that Anne should have saved the cost of drilling the new well by asking Tom to dig one by hand.

It was not merely coincidence that Tom's legal freedom from Shirley came through on the same day that he learned that Anne too was to become a divorcee. She had decided not to tell him until she had to, though she was not at all sure why she felt it unwise to do so. There was something about Tom which appealed to her. In trying to identify whatever it was, she saw him as something of a contradiction. He was rugged in some ways and rather weak in others. She suspected his upbringing and a mismarriage had a lot to do with his present nature. There was some depth to his character to which she might respond if he opened out. And if that person proved incompatible with her own reactions, then it might botch their business relationship to which she felt irrevocably committed. She now believed the farm-cum-nursery was a vital necessity for her own self fulfilment.

With so much else on her mind, Anne's few attempts at introspection always fell short of coming to a firm conclusion. Her mind became dazed as the sequence of events unfolded which she had to a large extent initiated. The Hemmings too had been influenced by moves she'd made and when Peter appeared in late August to say he had a problem, she wondered what else there would be to worry about.

'The babe is due in two weeks,' he told her hurriedly as if it was only two hours, 'and the vicarage will be ready for us next week. Your mother's agreed to sell us more or less all the bedroom furniture we've been using, which she doesn't want to take to Attleborough.'

'So you want some help moving it, eh?' Anne guessed.

'Yes, but there's more to it than that I fear,' Peter said with a deprecating smile. 'What she seems quite determined about is to temporarily move in with us, whether or not Claire's in the maternity ward by Monday week, and I can't refuse. I could fend for myself till Claire's up and about but your mother's idea is that she can bridge the gap and make it easier for Claire before she gets the call, and after she comes back from hospital. And then while she's with us, the furniture she does want can be sent to Attleborough.'

'A very neat arrangement,' Anne commented dryly, ' but there, mother always was an efficient organiser of both things and people. And is she hiring a van to move her things to Attleborough?'

'She hasn't said so, but when I said I'd ask you to move what we're taking from the farm she just frowned and said that was up to me. So, here I am, asking.'

Anne told him that with harvest almost done, she was sure it could be arranged. What she had to keep to herself was that she'd woken up that very morning with the impulse to offer to do much the same thing for Peter and Claire, but her mother had beaten her to it. In doing so Eileen had blocked up the bolt hole it would have been for her – to get away from the manor and Gerald's presence. She would, of course, still do so, but not until the farmhouse was practically stripped, and not for another two weeks.

Suddenly, as her spirits sagged, she felt the need to talk over her predicament with someone she could trust. There was Tom, and Ted Fletcher, who might be a better bet, but all he could do would be to offer to take her in till the dust settled. There was also Susan who was due home next day, having had a series of interviews for a job.

'I've got the one I wanted most,' Susan announced gaily. 'BBC – historical research and I'm due to begin in two weeks' time. Starting salary £9,000. Isn't that great!'

'Splendid,' Anne replied. 'And where will you live?'

'That's all fixed up too. They put me on to another girl who wants a flat sharer – Bernard Street, not too far away. Now mother, what about you?'

'Not very good I'm afraid. Let's go and get some tea and I'll tell you. We won't be disturbed in the kitchen. You realise the garden's open on Sunday? Last but one this year, now it's been extended to October as well.'

'Can't we opt out? Both you and me I mean?'

Half an hour later they had decided not only to opt out of being around for the Open Day, but to set off early Sunday morning in Susan's little car and head north for a fortnight's holiday together. They agreed happily to combine visits to gardens, along with Susan's preference for museums and places of historic interest.

In almost a fever of suppressed excitement, Anne made all the needful arrangements with Ted Fletcher and found herself almost asking permission from Tom to be absent from work.

'Do you good,' he said with a grin. 'And if you come back with some plants we don't have, it'll do me good too. As I've told you, my ambition has always been to have a thousand different kinds to catalogue. Do make sure you go to Edinburgh Botanic Gardens and places where they grow a wide range of perennials.'

Anne assured him she'd do what she could, but said she ought to take a copy of their own stock list now in alphabetical order. 'I'm more likely to do a swop, aren't I, than just beg for bits and pieces?'

'You're right again,' Tom chuckled. 'But even more important is to come back in one piece – both of you, I mean. And by the way, why not cut a spike of that Cimicifuga we're not sure about? They should be able to tell you at Edinburgh whether it's *ramosa* or *racemosa*.'

Chapter Fifteen

Although Gerald's short holiday near Moffat had been somewhat marred by rainy weather and his own meagre contribution to the bags of grouse, it had served to decide on his course of action. Divorce was the essential first step and Charlotte was obviously Anne's replacement, if she accepted his offer of marriage. If, as he now fervently hoped, Charlotte had been impressed with Melthorpe, then it would be the appropriate time to put the question.

Charlotte greeted him warmly on his return to the flat. She also told him in some detail how she'd lost her way, but came across the nursery first to find Anne quite affable. 'She even asked me back to tea, so I had the chance to see inside the house as well as the garden.'

'And what did you think of it?' Gerald asked softly with a smile.

'Charming, especially the house. Secluded but not hemmed in. Lots of character without being ostentatious. Needs to be lived in, of course, and if it were mine I'd never want to leave it.'

'It could be yours Charlotte.'

'How so?' Charlotte asked, wide-eyed, deciding to play it his way with more than an inkling of what was coming. 'You don't mean it'll be coming up for sale do you, surely . . . Anyway, I don't have funds enough to buy it, do I?'

'No,' he chuckled. 'I didn't mean it that way. You won't be surprised after what I've told you about Anne's defection that I'm suing her for divorce. It's the only solution and I'm quite sure she won't oppose it. Which means that in a matter of weeks I'll be free, and if you'll do me the honour, you can be mistress of Melthorpe Manor.'

For Charlotte the time for bargaining had come, because time was slipping away. None of the unattached men she'd met had appealed to her for what they could offer to meet her twin needs. Most of them could be more capable of giving her children than Gerald but none of them had a place in the country to compare with Melthorpe. In the circumstances, love was a very secondary factor. She had some affection for Gerald and could overlook most of his faults because she felt quite confident of her ability to hold her own. Anne had obviously failed to do just that and had seized the chance the farm had offered to gain her freedom. There was a risk that at his age he might fail to make her pregnant, but she'd already learned of a discreet insemination service available in case of need, which she would not hesitate to use.

'It would have to be conditional Gerald,' she whispered.

'Children, I suppose? I'd do my best Charlotte, and can say no more than that.'

'And play the father role?'

'Of course. Your happiness would be my first concern and I know what having offspring means to you. So that's settled, and we –.'

'Not quite Gerald. There's one other thing. You're old enough to be my father and there's a generation gap between us. I want you to be a real father to our children if we're fortunate enough to have any. If we're not, I may try to adopt, but what I don't want you to do is to be fatherly to me. That would be fatal to our relationship.'

Gerald stroked his little moustache. 'I think I know what you mean – and I don't think you need worry on that score. You'll have full control of the house, of course, and I won't stint your allowance just because you have money of your own. What more can I say?'

'You could say,' Charlotte said firmly, 'that you're offering me equal rights and equal say as your wife, in every aspect of our lives at Melthorpe. I don't mean "with all my worldly goods I thee endow", and all that crap in the marriage service. I mean a sharing partnership on an equal footing. I want to make it a real home base for your children too if they wish, but I couldn't if you insisted on making all the important decisions, which I suspect is what you've done in the past.'

Charlotte sat back and lit a cigarette. Gerald took it as a cue to select, trim and light a cigar. In the silence each fell back on their secret reservations, each confident that the discussion was academic in the belief that ultimate strength was on their side.

'It shall be as you wish, and I respect you for being frank. So – to put it baldly – it's a deal?'

'It's a deal Gerald. And if you want some practice for what's to come – let's go to bed early,' Charlotte said, standing up to give him a hearty kiss. Clutching his hands, she forced him into the waltzing position, which led after a couple of twists and turns to them both breaking out into convulsive giggling. And then, when Gerald was becoming out of breath, Charlotte pushed him on to the settee and draped herself over him, ruffling his thinning hair. 'That was fun,' she whispered.

'Wasn't it just,' Gerald gasped. 'I feel years younger than I've done for years – thanks to you.'

'And I think I know how to keep it that way. Begone dull care and all that, and to hell with convention. Tell me when Anne's gone and we'll begin as we mean to go on, eh?'

Gerald blinked, jerking his head back. 'Well,' he drawled with a broad grin, 'I don't see why not. There's no law against it so far as I know. But not a word to anyone until the coast is clear. I'll write to Julian and Susan and put them in the picture in good time. Pity you couldn't have met them, but never mind. They're old enough to know we've a right to live as we please. My dear, you don't know just what you've done for me. Now I don't even feel any grudge against Anne.'

There were no fanfares when, six weeks later, Charlotte arrived at Melthorpe as the new mistress of the manor. Because the wedding could not take place until Gerald's divorce from Anne was complete, it was best to keep a low profile. Charlotte had decided a spare bedroom should be hers rather than the one Anne had vacated, having almost emptied it of furniture when she moved to Dunsford at the end of September. The spare room was more convenient anyway, being next to Gerald's, but a new doorway had to be made to give her access to his bathroom. Charlotte's excitement and restless energy as she organised the move was very different from Gerald's cautious approach. For her, everything was falling into place because she'd made sure it would, and if sometimes he felt some resentment at being hustled, he tried hard not to show it.

One of the last things Charlotte did whilst still in the London flat was to have a pregnancy test. To have her suspicions proved correct added another dimension to her excitement. In one sense the news was calming, but it added greatly to her belief that she'd made the right decision in agreeing to marry Gerald. It mattered not at all to her that her baby would arrive a few weeks premature in the purely legal sense, but it did offend Gerald's secret scruples which again he had to keep to himself. But not for long, as Charlotte paid verbal tribute to his virile prowess, knowing it would never occur to him that she had privily supplemented the contribution he'd made with one from a sperm bank.

The first Sunday in October was the last of the season's Open Days. It was also the last which Charlotte spent at the flat. Had the weather been fine, Gerald would have taken it as a good augury, but even so the reduced numbers on a dull damp day spent over £300 on produce stalls in the outhouses. Having counted the total takings and decided on which charities to distribute the money to, he made out a list of what each had received over the whole season and sent it as a report to the Eastern Daily Press which published it in the weekend edition. It peeved him to note that only the total was mentioned in a short paragraph captioned, 'Melthorpe Manor Charities amount doubled'. Beneath were half a dozen lines in which his name was mentioned as the benefactor.

Charlotte, now settled in, was handed the weekly newspaper with Gerald's forefinger pointing to the place. 'I'd have thought,' he muttered, 'it was worth a bit more space after the extra advertising I did.'

'Perhaps they were short of space,' Charlotte smiled. 'That's a goodly sum but I expect you took off the advertising costs as an expense?'

'Of course, and more besides for other expenses, such as what was bought in for resale and what not.'

'Didn't you keep some for yourself? I would have done. At least I think I would,' she said gaily.

'Well,' Gerald drawled, 'I took nothing I didn't consider legitimate in the circumstances.'

'Such as what?'

'Oh, just a few items I'd otherwise not be able to have without being liable for tax.' Everybody avoided tax when and where possible, and Charlotte somehow encouraged him to be more open than ever he'd felt like being with Anne.

In another month he would seal their union with the quietest of Registry Office weddings. While he was so upset by Anne's behaviour, he'd not wished to let go. Now that he was secure as the husband Charlotte had sought in all but legal terms, Melthorpe meant much more to him with her there, and from now on he could happily shed his work load on to younger shoulders. To be just chairman for a few more years would be an ideal way of ripening off his very successful business career.

What Gerald saw as his well earned equanimity was however disturbed before the end of October by a letter from his London accountant. Would he please call next time he was in town as they wished to discuss with him a letter received from the Norfolk District Inspector of Taxes.

'Ah – major – do sit down,' said Mr Taplow handing over the letter in question. 'As you'll see, there are one or two questions I could not answer. The one about producing accounts for your garden openings to the public is the most disturbing.'

Having read it, Gerald handed it back saying that the Inspector had no right to pick on the newspaper report of the year's total of charitable donations. 'They can't call that trading,' he protested. 'It was purely for charity and what we sold was just surplus produce. I'll admit it came to almost as much as what was taken at the gate, but it makes no difference does it? I didn't bother to keep accounts because there was no need, when net proceeds were given away.'

'Hm! Well!' Mr Taplow demurred. 'The Revenue don't take that into account. Since I wrote to you I've looked up the tax laws on the subject and I'm afraid they have the right to claim tax on charitable donations of this nature, especially if sales to the public are involved. That comes within the category of trading, thus incurring tax liability.'

'But it's not trading! I won't have that Mr Taplow. Being open only once a month during the summer can't classify me as a trader. A trader would be just out for profit, surely? I never have been.'

'Believe me, major, I do understand how you feel, but what am I to tell the Inspector? I can't ignore him, can I?'

'I feel inclined to go and see him myself,' Gerald growled.

'I wouldn't advise you to do that. But can I tell him you will submit accounts for the past year? He might be satisfied with that, but I'm rather afraid he's more likely to ask for previous years as well.'

'And then what?' Gerald asked, his temper rising.

'That's a question I cannot answer with any certainty. It all depends on how far the Inspector is prepared to go. He might, for example, be willing to assess you for tax merely on this year's total paid to charities. Or he may well decide to do so on previous years as well. If you make an offer to do either or both – pleading ignorance of liability – he might accept your figures. But if you try to evade liability he can either demand full accounts for each year, or assess you on some figure of his own and leave you to come up with accounts to prove he's over-assessed your liability. It's not a pleasant prospect for you major, and I'll help you in any way I can if you'll entrust me. But frankly, I must advise you to declare everything, including all items you may have paid for out of the receipts which were in any way of benefit to you personally. I'd like to think that no such payments were made and that only legitimate expenses were deducted. You see, even cash paid to any of your regular staff for helping – over and above their wages – would be against the law for avoiding PAYE.'

There was no room for any other topic in Gerald's mind for the rest of that day. Anger and fear assailed him in turn with an overwhelming sense of injustice. He longed to tell Charlotte so much that the train journey back to Thetford station was more than usually tedious.

Whilst sympathising with his feelings and predicament, Charlotte seemed, he thought, reluctant to come out whole-heartedly on his side. This made him reflect for once that after all she was only a woman, and perhaps it was unfair to expect too much of her as if she were a paragon of judgment and support. For the first time she learned, little by little, just how much these open days meant to him, and how some of the garden equipment had been paid for from the takings.

'I think Gerald,' she said over coffee and liqueurs, 'that it's best if you can put yourself in both the accountant's and the tax inspector's shoes.'

'That's all very well Charlotte, but they won't see it as I do – from the charity point of view, I mean. I resent being dubbed a trader and being penalised for supporting charities.'

'Of course you do, and so would I if my motives were entirely altruistic. But I'd have to admit to myself at least that if I gained the slightest material benefit, then it would take some of the gilt off the gingerbread – wouldn't it?'

'But,' he persisted, 'I don't see any shame in gaining a trifle kudos – almost unavoidable I'd have thought, especially as it's in proportion to increasing donations.'

'But if it's against the law – and it seems it is – surely it puts you on the wrong foot when you know that not every penny of the takings has gone in donations. That's what they'll nobble you for if you're forced to admit it.'

Gerald gave a hollow laugh. 'You're talking the way Mr Taplow did, advising me to give in and pay up. I'm damned if I will.'

'Oh Gerald – please. I'm entirely on your side but I'm afraid you'll be damned if you don't give in and pay up. As I see it, you have no choice, and if you did plead ignorance and offer to pay the tax on what you've donated, it wouldn't break the bank would it? It would save you endless worry.'

Gerald gave little more than a grunt by way of acknowledgement. He could not admit to defeat. It was a matter of principle on two counts. One was on the score of equity; the other was that Charlotte, a woman, had touched a tender spot by pointing out that his motives had not been entirely altruistic.

'I'll find it hard,' he said after a long silence, just as Charlotte was about to switch on the television for the news, 'to muster up the same incentive in future, to have the garden open.'

She smiled back. 'I know, but there'll be other compensations by then, won't there? The babe should be here in early June.'

Charlotte went on to tell Gerald that she was longing to meet Julian and Susan and couldn't help wondering what their thoughts and reactions were on the radical change at Melthorpe. Above all, she wanted them still to regard it as home where they'd always be welcome. So far, she'd not met either of them and Gerald had thought it rather odd that she was against inviting them specially to meet her.

'Put yourself in their shoes,' she'd explained. 'Coming from me an invitation would put everyone of us on the spot. A request might appear like a command, as if I wanted to inspect them. It should be the other way round and I'm willing to be inspected when they feel like doing so. Doesn't that make sense?'

It had bothered Charlotte now and then to reflect on Anne's position compared with her own. She felt herself to be something of a usurper even though Anne had left the greater material comforts of the manor of her own free will. The thought of her living alone in the Dunsford farmhouse niggled sometimes to the extent of wanting to chat to her on the phone or, better still, go and visit her. But her own position in those first few weeks was too delicate. Gerald would certainly not have approved. And if she could get through to Susan, she hoped she'd find it possible to commend her wish to stay with her mother without prejudice creeping in. In her longed for pregnancy, Charlotte wanted above all peace and goodwill on all sides.

Chapter Sixteen

Those last few weeks had been hard for Anne to bear. She had made it clear that she would not oppose the petition and would have preferred to leave the manor for good on the day it was filed. But having no convenient alternative, she'd decided to stick it out until her mother left Dunsford. There were times when she felt a tremble of fear at the plunge she now had to take, but it was Eileen's implacable attitude which was a constant hurt. There were no grounds now for hoping that this attitude would soften, and even her insistence on staying at the vicarage was tantamount to a final slap in Anne's face. And it was not until Claire made it plain that she could cope, having brought a baby girl back from the maternity hospital, that Eileen took what odds and ends she'd left at the farmhouse and left for her new home in Attleborough.

On the first day that Gerald was away, with Tom and Ted Fletcher to help, Anne removed her personal belongings from the manor. When all was at Dunsford, she sat staring into the log fire and sobbed. Her familiarity with the house in which the first nineteen years of her life had been spent, was little comfort to her now. It had been a family home and now she was its only occupant. It was past midnight before she decided to go to bed.

Ted's wife Hilda came in most mornings for two hours to do the chores, but that did little to relieve her isolation. Foraging for breakfast next morning in the freezer Eileen had left behind, brought the need for shopping. The electric cooker too had been left, but she needed to buy smaller items of kitchen equipment as well as food to replenish the freezer. Having seen Tom and Ted about the work on hand she was about to drive off to Attleborough when Peter Hemming hailed her.

'I just wanted to tell you,' he said, 'how much we've felt for you over the past week or two. To be frank, we'd have much preferred to offer you sanctuary, but your mother is a very determined person and gave us no opportunity to refuse her when she said she'd come and help out.'

'That's all right Peter,' Anne smiled. 'I'm settling in now with the only regret that mother has disowned me. And of course it hurts.'

'We tried to soften her attitude towards you and perhaps it will sink in, given time. In making you feel isolated she's isolating herself, except that she's taken your husband's side and is still on good terms with him. I'd like to think – and so does Claire – that you'll still accept us as friends. Drop in whenever you feel like it for a meal or chat.'

One of these days, Anne told herself, she would call in on her mother and have it out with her. Back at Dunsford, she walked the short distance to the nursery and set to work. Tom had dug up eighty plants of the double-flowered Doronicum Spring Beauty. She divided them into over three hundred pieces, most of which he would plant at the weekend, but fifty were large enough to be sold next spring.

The more intimate Anne became with plants, the more their commercial value meant to her. There had been under twenty of this Doronicum which they'd moved from Melthorpe a year ago. Tom had divided them into eighty and already about fifty pounds worth could be sold in a few weeks' time. And in a year's time more than twice as many could be sold. Not all the kinds they grew increased so readily nor were sales guaranteed. There were costs to be deducted and there would very soon be Tom's wages to be charged against the nursery instead of to the farm. The nursery, she was resolved, must contribute to and not detract from the holding.

A love for plants had grown as the collection grew, revealing beauty and charm she had never been aware of before. But then had come the fascination of propagating them in the knowledge that they had an intrinsic value. And because they were specialising in the less common kinds, including some in the category of choice or rare, it brought a special incentive which enhanced both the aesthetic and the commercial aspects of the venture. It was rather odd, she thought, that for Tom value was centred more on rare and difficult subjects as being more worthwhile, whereas she put beauty and reliability first. But there, except for Tom's enthusiasm, devotion and skill, she would never have known plants offered scope for creative effort and expression.

Although Anne knew that Tom was longing to become a full-time nurseryman, he was quite stubborn in refusing to do so until the nursery was more extensive. Ted Fletcher reckoned that he could be spared from farm work early in the new year. Since Tom's daily work had been on the farm, he and Anne had spent relatively little time working together. He would tell her the next job to be done, show her if need be how to do it and then off he'd go under Ted's orders. His nursery work was in the evenings during the summer and at weekends when she'd been most often on duty at Melthorpe. Now that she was living in the farmhouse, her job as dark evenings came was preparing the catalogue, a task seldom needing help from Tom.

There were occasions when Anne thought Tom was unnecessarily brusque and impatient. Such occasions brought a reminder that their relationship as friends had veered towards a purely business partnership. The feeling of drifting along with Tom wherever the tide of events led, had given way to a separateness linked only by their mutual business interests. Her isolation had encouraged her to retreat into a kind of shell which made it more difficult to attempt to penetrate Tom's own shell of reserve. Even if she could bring herself to make the attempt and break through, she couldn't be sure what lay beneath.

Anne was well aware that since escaping from Gerald's domination she had let herself go, in the feminine sense. She'd never been at heart very clothes conscious and it was Gerald who encouraged her to be smartly dressed with care for her face and figure. For months now she had far more often worn jeans than a skirt and changed into a dress only on the evenings when Gerald was at home. Male garments were much more in keeping with nursery work and for that matter so was a more masculine approach to the farm and nursery.

By the end of October Anne was spending two evenings a week with the Hemmings. She was quite happy to talk babies and domesticity with Claire alone, then after a snack supper Peter joined them in discussions which she found lively and stimulating based as they mostly were on the book he was writing. He admitted that he'd deliberately chosen to minister to three small country parishes because it would give him time in which to write. Such a book, he said, required a vast amount of historical study and research which made the actual writing a very slow process. After two years he was barely half way, but two publishers he'd alerted were already interested.

'It seems,' he laughed, 'that books which swipe at the old Established Churches are much more saleable than those which support traditional beliefs.'

'But that's not the reason for writing yours, is it dear?' Claire was quick to defend him.

'Bless my soul, no! It's because I fervently believe the Church forsook basics once it became organised. But now people are no longer kept in the dark by priests, bishops and popes. They are no longer ignorant serfs beholden to the mighty and living in fear of hell fire. Scientific research had made the Bible suspect, and even the Gospels are open to criticism, which tell of tampering and revision to suit those who laid down doctrines and dogmas. What I'm trying to do is sort out what I see as the chaff from the grain, what is consistent with the essential message of Jesus – as the most divinely inspired teacher of all time.'

'Good for you Peter,' Anne whispered. 'And will you have something to say about women? I mean, how the Church carried on the old Jewish idea that women were inferior to men? Jesus never said so, did he?'

'No – and what he is reported to have said about divorce is, I believe, a later insertion – as was the command to make Peter the head of the Church. Lots of churchmen don't believe it either, but the higher they are in the hierarchy, the more they stand to be shot at from below. So they daren't rebel against the Establishment. But I dare, because as an ordinary country parson I don't have so much to lose. Nearly all the reformers in history have been upstarts from the ranks – like me.'

Anne found special interest in the subject of male-female relationship and most of all on the theme of Sukie Colegrave's book which she'd lent to Tom. Peter had also read it and reckoned that much more publicity should be given to the fact that each sex had an element of the other within them. He agreed that a better understanding of this and the need to know what made people tick was a way to wholeness of personality.

'What's amazing when one comes to think about it,' Peter went on, 'is that people who are able to discover so much about mechanics and physics have done so little to discover themselves as individuals. But there, I'm no better than anyone else because I can't be sure what part of me is my soul – or if in fact I have a soul at all. I feel I'm an awful hypocrite sometimes when I'm taking a service –

but not so much of a traitor because the urge to write this book is so strong – as if I were being compelled.'

'I'll be glad when it's finished,' Claire said.

But Anne decided to refer back to the subject of androgyny. Leaning forward with hands cupping her chin she asked if either of them ever felt the other sex element coming out – or wanting to.

'I can't say I have,' Claire replied. 'Nor would I say I'm a feminist. But I can say that having Sarah has done wonders for my femininity. And you must have felt that Anne with your two, especially when they were so dependent on you.'

'Up to a point, yes,' Anne conceded, 'but I also felt they should grow up to be individuals and not smothered by motherliness. But what about you Peter? Are you ever conscious of the feminine side of your nature?'

'Hm! – that's a poser. When I read the Spirit of the Valley I realised that what was argued so factually and forcibly must be accepted as true. And I still believe it is, but to work on it – apply it I mean – when so much of my mental energy is being soaked up in this book of mine that I seemed to lose my personality in it. I'd gone through a spell of self examination before I began it, to make sure I was tackling it with the right motives. I suppose if you want a direct answer to your question, I'll have to say no – I'm not conscious of a feminine part of my nature, though I still concede that it must be lurking somewhere inside me.'

'I'm only interested in the masculine side,' Claire said with a little laugh. 'I'd say let sleeping dogs – or rather bitches – lie.'

Peter laughed too, but Anne only smiled. He looked intently at her and then asked, 'Perhaps you're finding it difficult to come to terms with yourself? It wouldn't be surprising after the upsets and upheavals you've had. We'll be good listeners at least, if you'd like to talk about it.'

Although she'd brought the subject back into the discussion, Anne found herself reluctant to put into words some of the hazy thoughts she'd been having lately. All she had hoped for was that from an open three-sided discussion she would find it easier to see inside herself.

'Until about three years ago,' she began diffidently, 'I had no idea what androgyny meant, or that everyone is born with something of the other sex. Nor that the female was the basic sex. You see, I'd been brought up to feel – though I didn't fully believe it – that men were superior and that a woman's role was to be wife and helpmeet as well as mothering the man's offspring. And that's what I tried to be and do for over twenty years – from the age of nineteen when I married. Then, as you well know, I broke free. And having done so I found myself feeling – a queer feeling it was too, though I wasn't always conscious of it – that I was becoming less feminine. It came very slowly and at odd times, but since I began working with plants I sort of found myself letting go of my femininity. I wanted to be creative in what was more of a man's way of life – farm and nursery. There was no need to doll myself up once Gerald lost his hold over me and trousers were much more practical when I became a working woman and not the lady of the manor.'

She paused, thinking she'd said quite enough as she noticed how intent Claire and Peter had become. 'Most of the time,' she added, 'I'm concentrating on what I'm doing. It's only now and then that I see myself as having changed as a result of becoming my true self – if that's what's happening to me.'

Peter was obviously deep in thought but Claire suggested warily that it might be a case of adapting herself to a different kind of life which made her imagine she had become different. 'But I wouldn't say you really are,' she added. 'And if another man came into your life, you'd find the essential feminine was still intact. Don't you think so, Peter?'

'It might be so,' he said. 'But I don't feel we're competent to judge. A psychiatrist might be, and charge well for it. I'd say it's the nature-nurture syndrome – after what you've told us, Anne, about your upbringing and suppressing your inner feelings for so long. Cases of women finding fulfilment in creative work without the need for a man are not all that uncommon. It could be they have a stronger masculine element and it seems reasonable that in both sexes it varies from person to person, with some going all the way to a sex change – but one seldom hears of a woman wanting to change.'

'I've certainly no wish to do so,' Anne declared. 'And perhaps it's a fear of becoming too masculine if I don't check what seems to be that side of me coming out, which has set up a bit of a conflict inside me.' She paused, placing a finger on the tip of her nose. 'I wonder,' she continued, 'because I've just remembered something else in that book, and a bit I once read in The Guardian. It was about sex hormone production changing in the second half of life

– which tends to go in reverse – making women less feminine in some ways and men more so. Not that I've noticed much evidence in other people – older people – but apparently it's been proved. And at forty-four I must be in my second half.'

'Which goes to show,' Claire put in, 'that you needn't let it worry you. Just keep on being yourself, eh? And don't try to close your mind against the chances of another man coming along to share life with, without losing what you've gained the hard way.'

'Well said wife,' Peter laughed. 'And from little noises I can hear coming from a very young woman in a cradle, it's feeding time again.'

'And time for me to go,' Anne smiled, stretching as she stood up, an act which with her robust build made Claire appear slim and slight in comparison. Then she relaxed and gave Claire a kiss with a whispered, 'Thanks – both of you I mean. What you've said has helped. I'm beginning to feel it in my bones.'

The Hemmings had helped Anne to put the matter in some sort of perspective and she believed she had what it would take to prevent her from brooding over what might after all be a problem more imagined than real. What Claire had said about the effect of another man coming into her life had not sunk in. Chances of such a man appearing to spark off a romance were very remote in her situation. Nor did it appeal to her in the slightest. For one thing it would almost certainly shatter her ambitions to develop a nursery and the other factor was Tom Berkeley. She doubted if he would make a successful nurseryman on his own, lacking as he did some of the basic principles of economics – as she was discovering when pricing for the catalogue and the means of advertising it. There were occasions when she had to be patient and not show annoyance when he came up with out of date or impractical ideas on commercial aspects. What she saw last year of his working methods as the stamp of a perfectionist now sometimes appeared as his being rather pernickety, showing little concern for the principles of time and motion. It was odd that she, with no business experience, should have to be the one to decide for example not to offer certain kinds until stocks were larger. Tom would have catalogued everything – with the risk of having no reserves for another year. His excuse when she pointed this out, was that the more kinds of plants they offered, the better the response would be. And that he wanted to get the best return from the investment she'd made.

Being in the red at the bank did not worry Anne to any extent.

The manager had encouraged her to borrow the money for her mother's house, and if it took several years to come back into the black, it was her property along with the value of the farm. The bank overdraft was only a small fraction of her total assets. Eileen had paid no rent as laid down in the will, but it would be up to her mother to ask for more money if she needed it to live on. When the time came to visit her, it might be quite interesting to see how she reacted if Anne offered to supplement her income. It would be a case perhaps of heaping coals of fire on her obdurate head, from which years ago had come all those precepts and injunctions on a woman's proper role in life – subservient to men.

Chapter Seventeen

News had filtered through to Dunsford that Gerald had a lady staying with him. One rumour had it that they had been secretly married, another that she was a kind of housekeeper. But no one knew her name and because it was also said that Gerald was seen to go to London only once a week by train, two and two had been put together.

'Good luck to her,' Anne said cheerily, 'whoever she is. But no doubt all will soon be revealed.'

The whole truth did not come out until Christmas. Susan had come back and having stayed one night at the manor came to spend the rest of her break with Anne. She'd had somewhat mixed feelings and thoughts when news of Gerald's companion leaked through and was now agog to hear what Susan had to tell her.

'I think she'll be good for him,' Susan said soon after arriving at the farm. 'In fact, I spotted a change in Dad already. More human's the word, not so pompous. And they did marry secretly at a London Registry Office some weeks ago. And – wait for it Mum – she's preggers! Dad said not to spread it, but I couldn't keep it from you, could I?'

Wide-eyed, Anne said, 'Well, well, well! That really is news. But who is she, I'd like to know. None of the rumours there's been have answered that one. She must be quite young.'

'She's an "Hon". Mid-thirties I'd say. Sister of a man who lives in New Zealand and doesn't believe in titles. He inherited an estate – Marlington Hall, or some such name – and that's where Dad met her.'

'Charlotte Norton! Now it all fits in – or nearly all. She came here one day last summer, as a recent acquaintance of Gerald's, and –.'

Susan chipped in again and within a few minutes the whole truth including the flat sharing came out. Susan fancied the plot had been on Charlotte's initiative and insistence judging by the way

Gerald had sat almost meek and silent, with Julian listening with sometimes an incredulous look on his now bearded face. 'I've a notion,' Susan added, 'that by the time that baby comes – next June Charlotte said – Dad will be a changed man.' Susan then asked after Tom, giving Anne a quizzical look when she said there was nothing much to report.

'He still works hard,' she said, 'but is longing to spend more time on the nursery – hoping for lots of orders.'

'And what's he doing for Christmas? Have you asked him in?'

Anne said she hadn't but had been in two minds, partly because he wouldn't like to leave Mabel Adams alone. She was not very well and Tom did a lot for her about the house.

'Let's call in tomorrow,' Susan suggested. 'He might come if we both ask him, if only for a few hours, as it's Christmas Day. Maybe he'd come if we asked Mabel too. That fowl I saw in the fridge will easily feed four.'

When they called next morning Tom told them that he'd persuaded Mabel to stay in bed. She believed her headache and feeling cold were the first signs of 'flu and she'd refused to let him phone the doctor because it wasn't fair to expect him to come five miles on Christmas morning just for a touch of 'flu. Tom's deep-set eyes lit up when asked to join them for lunch, but he didn't think he ought to stay away for very long. 'I'm not sure it is 'flu,' he said, 'but if she's all right when I pop back after lunch, then I'd love to spend another hour or so with you. It's good of you to ask me and I wish Mabel had been well enough to come too, though she might have needed a lot of persuasion.'

Anne agreed, but any hopes she had of making him feel at ease as their guest did not materialise. Conversation over sherry and then lunch was rather stilted. When Tom returned after lunch, having checked on Mabel's condition, he said that he'd found her asleep and thought he could safely leave her for another couple of hours. During that time they talked about local affairs, the nursery and its prospects and Susan's work at the BBC. Tom went back to Mabel as dusk fell, but in less than ten minutes returned with the news that he'd found her shivering on the bedroom floor and scarcely conscious. He'd lifted her back into bed and rushed back to use Anne's phone to call a doctor. An hour later Mabel was on her way by ambulance to the little hospital near Attleborough. And ten days after that, Peter Hemming was conducting her funeral in Dunsford church, with Anne, Tom and Ted Fletcher amongst the score or so mourners who followed the coffin from the church to the open grave in the snow sprinkled churchyard. Apart from a niece and a cousin or two, Mabel's passing brought no other family mourners. Her only child had married an American airman and could not make the journey from California to attend.

Tom had elected to fend for himself whilst Mabel was in hospital. Susan had suggested after Mabel had gone that Anne should offer to take him in. But Susan did not and could not understand the peculiar relationship between her and Tom. Anne saw risks of closer company making for rifts in the nursery partnership and did not want to put the slightest pressure on him. It had to be entirely his choice. When Anne felt able to put the inevitable question to him, he said, diffidently, that he thought he'd prefer to carry on as tenant of the cottage at least for a time. If she wished to install another helper for the farm or whatever he'd understand and find lodgings. Already Ted's wife next door had offered, but he'd feel more freedom living alone – especially if Anne would be kind enough to add his wants to her shopping list. Anne felt that she could do no other than accept his decision as a clear indication of his preference for a bachelor, celibate existence. Perhaps his failed marriage was due to his inability to live in harmony with a woman. Not that if he had taken her offer to share the farmhouse with her, she would have expected or contrived a closer relationship to emerge, let alone flourish. For her, living alone in a five bedroomed house was far from ideal but she had to accept his right to live alone if that was what he wanted.

That January was a month of many weathers. It was quite frosty with a little snow at the time of Mabel's funeral, but then followed a mild, almost balmy spell which brought out the winter aconites and white tips to the snowdrops. Tom dug up plants for Anne to split and grade in the shed – astilbes, rodgersias and hostas. He planted the divisions for next season, and those selected in anticipation of spring sales were laid in close together. Conversation was almost entirely confined to their work.

On the last day of January a fierce wind blew up from the north east, bringing flurries of snow and low clouds. The temperature fell to below freezing, even by day, and the surface soil became hard with its crust of frost. The snow did not settle from the brief flurries but blew away to leave open ground bare. Tom could no longer plant and Anne had to use a fan heater to thaw out plants still to be divided, for frost had penetrated the wooden shed as well. And when those few trays full of plants had been thawed and split, then there would simply be no more work that she could do.

After a week's hard frost with Tom having to help Ted on hedge trimming, Anne was becoming fed up with nothing to do in the nursery. On Saturday afternoon she decided as a break from housework to seek the warmth and interest in the nursery greenhouse. There at least were cuttings and seedlings showing green growth in contrast to the sere, shrivelled stock outside. She went through the shed, attached for convenience next to the south end of the greenhouse, and let herself through the intervening door into the relative warmth inside. The greenhouse was low and narrow, the correct design Tom had said for propagating, with a narrow sunken path down two steps from the shed. Anne walked slowly, noting labels and stages of growth. A few, such as lavatera, were of autumn cuttings taken as reserve stock because older plants in open ground were not reliably hardy. The same went for penstemons and hebes and here they were, still green and some already calloused as the first stage for making new roots.

Anne was about half way along the thirty foot long narrow path when Tom also came in through the shed door. 'Brr! It's cold!' he said with a grim smile. 'I spotted you out of the kitchen window, but actually I came to get the barrow. I need some more firewood, if I may.'

'Of course you may. It's one of the perks. I've just noticed that some of the cuttings I took in October are on the point of rooting. What a good thing you asked me to do them as a precaution.'

'And so it was,' he added, 'to straw round the kniphofias outside. Frosts like this, with no snow cover are lethal for such things.' Inching along the path with weather, work and plants the only subjects of conversation, Anne reached the far end door with Tom close behind. 'Let's nip out quickly,' he said. 'The barrow's out there, but we mustn't let more cold air in than we have to.' The door opened inwards. Tom grabbed the handle as soon as Anne was through and on to the sloping ramp outside which did away with the need for steps at this end. She half turned as he closed the door and then stepped briskly up the ramp on which a little drifted snow had turned to ice. She slipped and as she fell heavily forward her feet knocked Tom's from under him and in an instant he was lying on top of her. He struggled to his feet, believing that she was waiting for him to do so first. She'd let out a loud 'Ow!' as she fell, that was half a shriek and half laugh. But now she did not move and made no sound. Tom went down on hands and knees and with a stab of anxiety realised her head had hit the icy concrete path hard enough to knock her out.

'Oh – Anne – Anne!' he whispered as he tried to put an arm around her shoulders, bulked by her padded anorak. He managed to turn her face upwards but found that he could not lift her in the narrow, slippery space.

'Anne, Anne, please wake up!' he repeated, his face close to hers. A little blood oozed from a patch on her forehead just above her left eye. He pulled back her woolly hat and gently pushed a lock of hair away from the wound. Then, bending double, still on his knees, one arm keeping her head off the path, he kissed her forehead whispering, 'Anne – Anne!' catching his breath with sobs. And as his kiss lingered, her grey eyes opened and blinked with a flutter. 'Oh Tom,' she whispered. 'How silly of me. Should have been more careful. Must have blacked out—.' She put a gloved finger to her forehead. 'It's blood, and it hurts!'

Tom was already helping her up. Standing behind he lifted her into a sitting position on the path and then with another heave on to the low side wall of the ramp. Then he sat beside her. 'Must get you in the warm,' he muttered. 'It's my fault Anne for not warning you – making you hurry.' Then he took off his overcoat and wrapped it around her, supporting her back with his arm. 'I know a better way of getting you back to the farm than trying to get the van over the frozen ruts – if you'll let me.'

'I don't mind how I get back Tom – but I'm a bit too shaky to walk and my ankle hurts too.' Her voice was a little stronger now. The barrow stood upside down just behind them. It was an old type wooden one made for nursery work with a flat bottom. Tom righted it. 'If it's not too undignified, it'll do as an ambulance,' he grinned.

'It'll be a new experience for me,' Anne said with a little giggle.

Tom helped her on to her feet and holding her close edged her to the barrow. 'Sit well back and hold on to the sides and let your legs dangle when I move off. I'll go very slowly till we get on to a smoother roadway.'

The first fifty yards was uneven and as Tom slowly pushed his load avoiding hard frozen bumps and ruts, Anne sat sedately back as bidden, alternating winces with giggles. Passing behind the cottages, Tom steered on to the path leading to the farmhouse which was still two hundred yards away, well back from the road – the one Anne used when going to the nursery. In turning one corner Tom slipped and nearly tipped the barrow over. Anne suggested a pause, knowing that her weight was no easy load, but he went grimly on. By the time they reached the back door, Tom's shoulders and arms were aching.

'I can hobble in,' Anne said wincing as her feet touched the ground, 'but I'll need you to steady me. I don't fall lightly do I?'

Tom steadied her with an arm under her shoulders and having gained the doorstep he pushed the door open. He slipped off his own coat from her shoulders letting it fall on the floor. Then he gently eased her onto the settee and lifted her legs as she slewed herself into position. Anne sighed with relief as he arranged a cushion for her head, saying that he'd make up a good fire, boil the kettle and make tea before bathing her forehead. 'If you'll let me of course, or would you rather I phoned the doctor?'

'Not necessary. I'll let you be nurse Tom.'

He turned, about to go into the kitchen. 'Tom,' she whispered.

'Yes – what?'

'You kissed me, didn't you – when I was coming to?'

He gave a half nod with eyebrows raised. 'I hope you –' he began, but Anne cut him off.

'Before you begin nursing,' she smiled, 'come and kiss me again.' Haltingly at first, he came closer and then, suddenly, he dropped on to his knees beside her, clasped her hand and kissed her cheek while she put her spare hand behind his head drawing him, holding him, till their lips touched. 'Now you can go,' she whispered in his ear, 'but not for long. I need you.'

'God knows,' Tom muttered, his eyes moistening, 'how I've loved you – from afar – but didn't think you needed me.'

'You silly man! Make my tea strong and sweet, then you can bathe my forehead.'

With a lighter heart than he'd had for years, Tom made up the lounge fire from the log basket and with more haste than speed found tea, crockery, a basin and cotton wool, calling back now and then to Anne to ask where such things were kept. In between her sips of tea he tenderly dabbed round the broken skin on her forehead, now swollen, but not bleeding. Apologising again, she commended his gentle touch but asked for Anadin to ease the aching pain. 'Now my ankle,' she said, 'It's the left one. Ease my boot off slowly, it feels rather swollen.'

He unlaced her fleecy lined boots and very gently eased them off as if both ankles were sprained. Anne said a cold compress was supposed to be the right treatment and Tom was quick to respond. 'But – what about your –.'

'My tights? No problem at all. I can't take 'em off and nor can you. But you'll find some scissors in the first aid cabinet and you can clip the left foot off, can't you?'

With an effort she lifted and twisted her left leg and turned back the bottom of her trouser leg. 'There we are,' she laughed. 'All ready for you, but getting my jeans and tights off at bedtime won't be so easy.'

Five minutes later he was holding a cold water soaked teacloth over her ankle whilst Anne fidgetted between little gasps of pain, trying to choke them back. She told him not to bandage her ankle and then pulling the settee nearer the fire and drawing the curtains he squatted down on a pouffe beside her and stroked her outstretched hand.

'What about that barrowload of firewood you were going to get?' Anne said with a provocative smile.

'What about it?' he countered.

'What I mean is,' she chuckled, 'are you going to get it and leave me now that you've done your first aid nursing?'

Tom gave her a puzzled look as if unsure what she was getting at. 'I don't want to leave you Anne, and you did say you needed me –'

'So I do Tom – so I do. I don't want you to leave me – ever.'

'In that case,' Tom whispered, 'I'll go and fetch a barrow load of my things from the cottage. I want nothing better than to be with you – always.' Then he kissed her hand before holding it up to his cheek where it caught a tear.

Busy though he was for the next two hours, Tom was in a deep sense of wonderment. Not quite a daze because there was so much to do. It was as if all his long standing inhibitions and frustrations had blown away like leaves in an autumn gale. In their place was an uplift of spirit, which he could feel in the pit of his stomach with the thought that Anne needed him. Not just for business reasons or for what other service he could perform for her materially, but as a man. And it was a two way need – his for her, hers for him. The feeling of unworthiness which had made him keep what he felt battened down, to the point of being sometimes brusque with her, was now replaced by subdued elation. He knew now that she had loved him in spite of his shell of reserve. In his sudden euphoria, of emotions released, he could have cheerfully become Anne's slave. But he knew well enough that what she wanted to see and live with, was his true self. At last had come the chance for them both to become whole personalities – giving and taking, loving and living fully.

It was with these thoughts dominating that Tom waited happily for sleep that night in the bedroom Anne had assigned to him, next to hers. She had gone to bed early and he'd helped her up the steep stairs backwards, sitting down on each step. Before slumping on the bed she'd unzipped her jeans which he'd eased off her legs. The sight of her snuggled under the duvet ten minutes later when he brought her a mug of Ovaltine brought another surge of emotions and of love that almost hurt. 'Leave the door ajar,' she whispered when he'd kissed her goodnight.

Chapter Eighteen

When the frost began to give way, weather-wise Ted Fletcher remarked that a 'slow thaw was a sure thaw'. And so it proved, just as the first orders for plants came in the mail. So far more than a hundred catalogues had been sent off to enquirers. It was not a sumptuous affair but although only pocket-sized, the front cover was in colour featuring a panoramic view of the nursery at its most colourful period. Seventy odd orders were received in February which, Tom and Anne agreed, was significant. Even more significant was that the average value of orders came close on £10, and it augured well for success.

Anne was so conscious of her changed attitude to life that she fancied it could be an act of providence that things had suddenly fallen into place for herself and Tom. She liked to think it was, and decided to ask Peter Hemming's opinion on the matter. His reply was not what she'd hoped or expected coming from a parson.

'If that's what you feel,' he smiled indulgently, 'then hold on to it as long as you can. My head tells me it's coincidence – that God doesn't interfere with human affairs. If he did, then we'd have to believe the tragedies as well as the benefits were due to divine intervention, wouldn't we? I believe God has given us free will and, basically, the old saying that God helps those who help themselves is true – but risks are always lurking.'

'Hm! That's not what the Bible says, is it?' Anne protested.

'No, but one has to be realistic. Which reminds me, are you going to let me marry you and Tom? It would give me a lot of pleasure to splice you.'

Anne blushed and then laughed. 'We've been too busy to discuss it. But it's not a bad idea – and realistic as you suggest. I'll see if Tom is willing to share his name – which I'd prefer anyway to the one I have.'

Anne and Tom had been living together for a month, and they had been very busy. It was their policy to despatch orders within twenty-four hours of receipt, in the belief that customers should not be kept waiting. On top of order despatching, there was spring propagating for Anne and planting for Tom, now on full time nursery work. In the evenings, sometimes until quite late at night, there was the necessary paper work to be done. It was not, they began to realise, going to be a hugely profitable business, though Tom was more optimistic than was Anne – who was keeping the accounts. But it was a satisfying enterprise and when a few letters came complimenting them on quality, good packing and prompt service, there was all the justification they needed to expand both in variety and quantity. Anne foresaw that by next autumn, if not before, more help would be required, and that would reduce the profit margin unless they overcame their reluctance to increase prices.

Peter Hemming married them early on Easter Monday morning with only Susan, Ted Fletcher and Claire as witnesses. No bells, no music, no fuss, and by mid-morning when Susan left them, Anne and Tom were back at work on the nursery. Yet somehow news of the wedding had reached Melthorpe by evening, for Charlotte telephoned to offer her congratulations and good wishes.

Anne beamed. 'Next to becoming Mrs Berkeley,' she told Tom, 'that was the nicest thing that's happened today.'

'Maybe the major will do the same for me,' Tom smiled back.

'No fear of that Tom. But Charlotte said he was in fine form, whatever that may mean. Charlotte has a very strong personality and Susan's noticed a big difference in him. It's marvellous, don't you think – to have no hard feelings against anyone? And Susan has tipped me off about mother. I've had to hold myself back from going to confront her ever since I moved in here, for fear of making her more upset. Susan saw her yesterday and says she's softened quite a bit. So, the time is ripe and now I'm a married woman again let's hope she'll accept me back as a daughter. It's the one fly in the ointment for me.'

Tom told her that he too had no hard feelings against anyone. But as his mind ranged round it came to rest on Sandra, with a longing he decided he must keep to himself. This was his one fly in the ointment. He'd heard nothing of her for nearly two years, lacking what it would take to contact Shirley who might know where and how she was.

Later in April, Anne called on Eileen after shopping in Attleborough. 'I was wondering,' Eileen greeted her complainingly, 'how long you'd be before you came to see me. I was beginning to think you'd disowned me. But better late than never.' There was a vestige of a smile in her eyes.

This was enough to break the ice for Anne. 'Oh mother!' she said giving her a hearty hug and kiss. 'I thought you'd disowned me! And now that I'm happier than I've been for over twenty years, I couldn't bear to think you –.'

'Nor could I,' Eileen broke in. 'And how's that nursery business going?' Question after question came during their cups of tea, with Eileen carefully avoiding any suggestion or interference that she'd been to blame for the rift between them. Nor did she refer again to Tom, as if he was a mere accessory to the fact that Anne had come back into the marital state which she should never have left. But Anne guessed that Gerald's conduct had paved the way towards her taking a more lenient view of her own. Her mother, she deduced, had seen him as above reproach, but once she'd learned that he too had offended her code of marital fidelity and respectability before marrying again, it put a different complexion on Anne's behaviour.

'All's well,' Anne announced to Tom on her return. 'And next time you'll have to come with me to be inspected – and approved of.'

'I'll feel safe so long as I'm with you,' Tom said.

That feeling of safety, Anne reflected, was mutual. She had long since discovered that in many respects hers was the stronger personality of the two. Tom had different strengths, but what had struck her forcibly since they came to live together was how her initiative and determination seemed to inspire him to become more positive himself. It was not that she had to prod him but a case of her sparking off in him the kind of response which brought her a respect and at times admiration for him, making their joint effort dovetailed and strong.

When they came together in bed at night it was as a result of his interpretation of her need for him. A certain smile or gesture became as effective as a spoken word or hint that she would welcome him as bedmate. Right from the first time they made love, she had sensed that it was up to her to take the lead. Tom's timidity would certainly emerge if she waited for him to rouse her. That was supposed to be the man's role and Gerald had always practised it, though he'd never generated much by way of spontaneous reaction from her. With Tom it was very different. She made the approach and he made the kind of response which brought a united effort to give each other everything they possessed. The utter contentment after love-making as well as the ecstasy of the act itself was, Anne believed, abundant proof that her role as leader was right. That it might be due to her streak of masculinity, her animus merging with Tom's anima, was a matter for rejoicing and far removed from an abnormality. It was good, so good that it must be proof also that the androgyny factor in them both was an enhancement to their relationship in the sexual sense as well as in other ways. It was something to cherish and not to squander by over-indulgent frequency. It was their secret which made a power of difference to their relationships with other people as well as to their partnership in business.

It was the end of May before all the planting was finished. But in spite of having sold more plants than they had dared to hope in their first season, there was no improvement in the nursery bank account. Not that either of them were worried because the reason for considerable extra expenditure was there to see. There were nearly a hundred additional species and varieties of plants they had acquired from far and wide, and there was an electric pump in a little shed over the artesian well. This had been installed in April along with underground mains, feeder pipes and sprinklers, enough to cover four acres of the field. A dry spell in early June brought them into use and Anne reckoned it was worth the cost just to see how the plants perked up under the fine, misty spray.

Selecting new acquisitions for stock purposes was no longer Tom's sole prerogative as it had been. The choice was now jointly made as the two of them studied books and catalogues during the winter evenings. Anne had broken through the barrier which botanical names had formerly presented to her. Having grasped the principles of pronunciation, many names held some meaning for her and she was able to an increasing extent to relate descriptions to adaptability of given subjects to the soil and situation on the nursery.

By the end of June the first trickle of visitors had begun. Most of them had written previously for a catalogue but had not placed an order. Now, it seemed, they were still interested but preferred to see for themselves before ordering what the Dunsford Perennials' catalogue stood for as plants came into flower. Although visitors scarcely averaged one a day, they had a nuisance value as well as a commercial one. Tom artfully suggested Anne should be the one to show them round whilst he continued hoeing or planting, but she too felt some suppressed resentment at having to neglect her propagating. After a few such interruptions which seldom resulted in a firm order for later despatch since open ground plants could not be dug up until September, she began smilingly to invite people to walk round on their own, make notes and ask questions when they had done so.

On the last Saturday in June, a decrepit little Ford edged in to the patch of gravel which served for parking. The occupants, a young couple, emerged slowly under Anne's watchful eye through the potting shed window as if they were unsure if they'd come to the right place. Very unlikely customers Anne thought as she decided to carry on with her batch of aster frikartii cuttings – half hoping the couple would retreat. But they shuffled towards the shed and when they appeared at the open door she turned with, 'Can I help you?'

'Well, we were looking for Mr Berkeley,' the girl said, who appeared barely out of her teens. 'We were told this was his nursery.'

'He's hoeing some distance away,' Anne told her with curiosity aroused. 'I'm Mrs Berkeley, if that's any help.' There was, she noticed, a look of appeal in the girl's eyes but the young man was peering around as if interested.

'He may be surprised to see me – 'cos my name's Sandra Berkeley. I'm his daughter.'

'He'll be surprised all right – and pleased. I'll take you to him. I'm pleased to see you too. Come on both of you.'

Tom spotted them and Anne waved to come over. Within minutes both Tom's and Sandra's eyes were watery. Anne drew the young man aside to walk along the path. He gave his name as Mark Freeman. In the few minutes they had together he told her that they were not married and that the baby they'd left in the car was not his. He had recently been made redundant and although he'd like to marry Sandra, it paid them not to. At Sandra's request they had come up for the day to Norfolk from Uxbridge and had called first to see Shirley, who told them where to find Tom.

'This is marvellous,' Tom said when the four came together again. 'Absolutely marvellous. I expect Mark has filled you in, Anne? But there's a lot more we'd like to know, so – let's –.'

'Let me finish putting my cuttings in and then I'll join you,' Anne interrupted.

'Can I watch you?' Mark asked. 'I've never been on a nursery before – got stuck in an office job and now made redundant by a computer.'

Anne rode in the car with him to the farm after glancing at the baby boy in the carrycot on the rear seat. Tom and Sandra had walked the shorter way.

'I met Sandra on a bus,' Mark told her, 'saw she was pregnant and guessed she was in trouble – like me, 'cos it was the day I got the push.'

'And you've been together ever since?' Anne suggested.

'Yep! It only took me a week to decide she was the one for me. She told me she'd gone a bit wild like, but – well, I believed her when she said the baby coming put her straight, and I knew she'd be okay for me when she said she wouldn't have an abortion.'

Later, when Sandra was feeding the baby, Tom told Anne much the same story coming from Sandra. Shirley, it appeared, wasn't all that pleased to see her turn up at her pub. 'She was busy with customers coming in for lunch so they had a snack in Attleborough and came on here. Sandra says she never did blame me except she thought I ought to have stood up to Shirley more. Did you get much out of Mark?'

Anne told him what she'd learned. 'He's twenty-six and seemed quite interested in the nursery. Even watched me making cuttings. Now he's looking round the farm buildings. A thought has just occurred to me. He's obviously hungry for a job, and Mabel's cottage is still empty. Ted was saying only last week we ought to find a tenant.'

'Are you really saying that they can have –.'

'Yes Tom, that's what I'm saying.'

'You never cease to amaze me Anne –' Tom said, pressing her hand between both of his. 'It'll be taking a risk,' he added, 'but I'm pretty certain they will jump at the offer. I'd make sure Mark knows he'll have to work hard and learn fast.'

'Don't say anything to them yet Tom,' Anne warned. 'Let's tell them more about the nursery – or you can. Show Mark round while I talk to Sandra. Then I'll put it to them when we're all together again, if you think Mark's okay as the other helper we know we'll have to take on very soon.'

Two hours later Sandra, her baby and Mark left with both Anne and Tom waving them goodbye. 'Take care! See you again soon!'

'It's been a red letter day for me,' Tom said fervently.

'And I believe it's going to work out,' Anne rejoined. 'I've been niggled about the cottage being empty since you left, but – well, I just had a kind of hunch it would fill a need if we didn't hurry to get in a new tenant. Ah! There's the phone ringing.'

Tom followed and could hear her saying, 'Yes, of course. I'd been hoping to hear from you, but I can well understand. Yes – see you about five. That's fine.'

'You'll never guess who that was,' Anne smiled as she hung up.

'No, but it sounds as if we haven't finished with visitors for the day. It's four thirty so whoever it was hasn't got far to come.'

'It's Charlotte – Potts, as it is now, would you believe?'

'Wonders never cease,' Tom muttered facetiously. 'What's she coming for – or is it a courtesy call?'

'I fancy it's more than that,' Anne said. 'She's been wanting to come over ever since her twins were born, but couldn't until she got some reliable help. Now she has and I wouldn't be surprised if she wants to see flowers. That was the impression she gave me.'

The twins, a boy and a girl, had arrived nearly a month ago causing many comments round about, following so soon after the gossip fodder both Gerald and Anne had already provided. What became morning news in either Melthorpe or Dunsford had travelled over the three miles distance well before evening. The divorce had been anticipated in advance of it becoming official, but no one had imagined the new Mrs Potts would be so promptly in the family way – much less to present the major with twins.

Charlotte had known at five months, but had prudently kept it to herself until near the end of her time. She'd not even told Gerald. And when twins arrived his sense of achievement was boundless, although he gave full credit to Charlotte for her part. That they were not identical twins in no way detracted from his pride and joy, for they gave proof of his virility, rare indeed for a man of nearly sixty. It was also proof of his good judgment in choosing such a person as Charlotte to replace the wife who had let him down.

But now he had no hard feelings, and as the generous side of his nature surfaced again it centred on Charlotte who had done so much for him. She had also saved him a lot of anxiety over his tax problem. Having agreed on Charlotte's recommendation to pay the Inspector's demand for eight thousand pounds, they had waived their right to prosecute him for evasion and making inadequate tax returns. As a result, his enthusiasm for opening to the public had waned. And if Charlotte really preferred a less formal type of garden, then shrubs and perennials would be much less troublesome than bedding out two or three times a year.

Charlotte had not openly persuaded him to have done with the Edwardian tradition in gardening. All she'd done was to express a wish for more variety, pointing out that a once-off investment in shrubs and perennials would last a lifetime, with very little maintenance. This fact he'd always known but had felt it to be almost a duty he should fill those box-edged geometric shaped beds – probably a century old – with the kind of flowers for which they were intended. It was all right to let the public see them but now he felt that he didn't need public approval. It was, after all, a private garden. He knew the names of the score or so kinds of bedding plants he'd grown but to be asked the botanic names of a wide range of other plants and shrubs would be no pleasure at all. Quality rather than variety had been much more satisfying, but now it was time to make changes if only because it would please Charlotte. If she so wished, he told her, she could go over to Dunsford and make a selection and ask Berkeley's advice if need be. He knew the manor garden well enough, but although he had no hard feelings towards him and Anne, he'd prefer not to be involved again with either of them, in any way.

'It shall be as you wish Gerald,' Charlotte smiled.

Charlotte arrived promptly at five. She found Anne weeding a narrow border which had served for a flower garden ever since she could remember.

'Hello!' Charlotte greeted breezily. 'I wished I could have come before now, but what with one thing and another – you know –.'

As they shook hands, Anne just said, 'You're very welcome.'

'Thanks – it's more than I deserve. You must have thought – after what's happened since my visit last August – that I came then under somewhat false pretences. No hard feelings I hope?'

'None whatsoever – against you or anyone else. You could scarcely have acted otherwise, could you?'

'Well, no,' Charlotte persisted, 'but at the time you must have felt out on a limb.'

'All over now,' Anne laughed. 'And I hope you're happy too. What are the twins' names?'

'Andrew – Gerald's choice, and Caroline – my choice. Now, to business, because I really do need some advice. I'd like to take a quick look at your nursery, but when it comes to placing an order for plants, I'd like to leave the selection to you – and Tom, is it – your husband? I've persuaded Gerald to have done with most of the summer bedding. And if your advice would be to scrap those horrid little box hedges, then I'm pretty sure this'll be their last year. But of course it'll have to be entirely my own idea – with reasons why.'

'Understood,' Anne smiled. 'And I know Tom would recommend it. They're one reason why I could never take much interest in the garden there. Much too formal – well, nuff said on that score.'

'We'll need shrubs as well as perennials – and here comes the next question. Would you and Tom, with my connivance at least, be willing to design a new lay-out – or would you rather I commissioned a garden architect to plan what should go where?'

'That's a tricky one,' Anne mused. 'What I could say is that I'd like to have a go, but I can't speak for Tom – though I'm pretty sure he would row in. At least we know the site well enough. But you'd want to have a share in the planning surely? And what about Gerald? I can't imagine a foursome agreeing.'

'I think,' Charlotte said, 'that Gerald's in the mood to chuck tradition overboard. He may want nothing to do with it – but it'll be up to us to make sure it's a success – enough to stimulate a new interest and give him no grounds for regrets. Who's to do the planning is the big question and it struck me that you two, with me sort of carrying the can so far as Gerald's concerned, could do it as well as an architect who probably wouldn't know as much about plants as you do.'

By this time they had met up with Tom on the nursery just as he'd finished watering the frames. Once Anne had explained, he was all in favour. 'So long as Anne's willing to, I certainly am – as a planning trio based here. We all know the site well enough. And I hope the major will have each kind properly labelled – so he too can study the botanic names. It's the only way to become interested.'

'Splendid!' Charlotte said with a little handclap. 'And speaking of names – legally I'm Charlotte Potts, but socially I've decided to be Charlotte Sporle – just Charlotte to you, of course. The Sporles originated from the Norfolk village of that name – but I'll drop the meaningless "Hon".'

'Why not?' Anne said. 'I sometimes wished I could have stuck to my Webley surname. But now I'm very content with Berkeley.' She gave a warm smile at Tom, sidling up to him. Then Charlotte added, 'and did you know Berkeley is one of the oldest Anglo Saxon names on record? Doesn't that make you feel proud?'

'I couldn't feel any prouder than I do already,' Tom smiled.